BEOWI
AND Thꞓ
Dragꝍn
Raiders

TRANSLATION BY
PROFESSOR
BURNS-LONGSHIP

MØGZILLA

BEOWUFF AND THE
Dragon Raiders

First published by Mogzilla in 2012

Paperback edition:
ISBN: 9781906132392

www.mogzilla.co.uk

Printed in the UK

Thanks to: Michele, Scarlet, Jon, and Luke.

PROLOGUE

The moon peeps out from behind the cloud-murk. The long-fire blazes in the pit. All of you Carls and Thanes sit in your King's hall, ready to hear a tale that will help to see off the night.

Beowuff's tale begins in a barrel. Beowuff is me, by the way, in case the weak-wits amongst you were wondering. You can be sure that this story will make poor Beowuff look less of a Lord-dog than the heroes you'll find in all the other sagas. Why? Because Beowuff will run from the field of war and he'll push other dogs into danger's jaws to save his own neck from the raiders' axes. He'll lie and cheat his way through this saga from start to finish, like he always does. Only this time, he'll even sell his bench-mates to their worst enemies, so he can get his thieving paws on a heap of monk-gold and treasure.

So sup up your meat-mead and lift up your ears and get ready for the tale of:

Beowuff and the Dragon raiders.

CHAPTER ONE

DRAIN-MAKER

How long I lay in the 'fish-bath' I cannot say. What is the fish-bath? Well, as every young pup should know, 'the fish-bath' is another word for the sea. A 'kenning' we call them where I come from. Where a ship is never a ship, it's called a 'sea-cutter'. A friend is called a 'bench-mate' and a battle-axe is known as a 'head-taker'. But there's no time for kennings now. I must take to tale-telling like a pirate takes to plunder.

We bobbed about in a barrel, my bench-mate Arnuf and me. Long time we held on, through swells and gales until we sank into a whimpering sleep while the storm-Lords shook us to pieces.

When we awoke, the sea was butter-smooth and as grey as fire-pit ash. We found ourselves washed up on a strange shore. The wind felt warm on my muzzle and my coat dried in moments under the kind sun.

I staggered up and looked around. A river snaked into the sea. Wild-fowl flocked in their hundreds. Fat little fish swarmed like bees in the shallows. Red deer danced on the hillside. The land was covered in ancient forest with sticks a plenty and rabbits – I tell no word of a lie – rabbits the size of badgers! Lined up in rows, ready to be chased. I could hardly believe my good fortune.

'This is nice,' said Arnuf, shaking the sea-grit out of his coat.

5

'Nice?' I growled. 'Nice? Is that all you can say to describe this Wunderland? It's glorious! It's like Valhalla, without the fighting.'

Arnuf twisted his muzzle, looking puzzled. I ignored him and trotted along the beach, staring out to sea. The water seemed to turn a shade bluer every time I looked at it.

'This place is just like home,' said Arnuf. 'Back in Gutland, we have the best beaches in the North.'

'If you like stone-choked shores,' I laughed.

Arnuf growled.

'Come on!' I laughed. 'Gutland's beaches are wretched. They look like something the Ice-Giants spat out at the beginning of the world.'

As we crested a dune, the view opened out and I spotted a figure wearing a brown cloak.

'Gutland has its good points...' began Arnuf.

'Shut your snout-hole!' I ordered. 'I've seen a local. Now be silent and watch a master at work.'

We approached to find a dour-faced dog, digging in a ditch. He was caked in mud and filth from nose to tail.

'Better not get too close,' I warned. 'He might have the plague.'

'I thought you said this was Valhalla,' said Arnuf. 'Do they have the plague in the next world?'

With a sudden bound, the figure sprang out of the ditch. He was dressed in a cloak, knotted at the waist and he wore wooden cross-sticks on a rope at his collar. Matted fur poked out from below his hood. Words cannot describe how he stank. The stench he gave off would have scared the flies out of a pirate's pest-hole.

'Stay back Arnuf,' I warned. 'He's got the mange, by the smell of him.'

'Greetings,' he called. 'I am Brother Clodus.'

'Oh! I've always wanted a brother,' yapped Arnuf in excitement.

'He's not YOUR brother! He's a monk, you bog-brained bone-head,' I snapped.

'A monk?' gasped Arnuf. 'Beware! For I've heard they can be vicious when they're cornered.'

Arnuf reached for his knife and growled at the poor bewildered Brother.

'What in the name of the Bearded Bonefather do you think you're doing?' I asked.

'Trapping him, so I can skin him,' explained Arnuf. 'We'll get a good price for his furry pelt. I hear that all the royal ladies like to line their collars with monk.'

'He's a monk, not a mink! You knife-happy nit-brain! Surely you've heard of monks before? They're the quiet fellows who live together in packs in monasteries.'

Arnuf still looked puzzled. I carried on explaining, though I knew it would do little good. 'You know, monasteries – those quiet places with the little huts that look like stone bee-hives. Don't tell me you've never looted a monastery?'

'Never,' he declared.

'Thunder-sticks!' I snarled. 'You don't get about much do you Arnuf? Well listen, monasteries are places where packs of monks live together, digging their fields and brewing tasty mead to drink. They also sit about all day mumbling prayers to their gods.'

'We pray to god,' corrected the Brother. I noticed him touch the little wooden cross-sticks at his collar.

'Sorry Brother!' said Arnuf, putting away his knife. 'I thought your pelt looked a bit scratchy.'

'That's his 'cowl', not his pelt!' I corrected. 'It's a kind of a cloak that monks wear. It's also called a 'habit.'

'Well it's a filthy habit,' said Arnuf. 'With all of that pit-digging he's been doing. Don't you hate working in that ditch Brother... er what did you say your name was?' asked Arnuf.

'Brother Clodus,' answered the monk. 'And if you must know, I neither like it nor dislike it.'

'I see,' said Arnuf. 'That bad eh?'

'You misunderstand me,' muttered the monk. 'I neither like nor dislike clearing dirt from the drains.'

'No wonder you stink!' said Arnuf. 'It's terrible work Brother, is muck-raking.'

The poor monk looked vexed. I didn't blame him. Talking to Arnuf for more than a moment would bore a starving bear back into its cave in springtime.

'Muck-raking as you call it, is the work that I have been given,' sighed Clodus. 'Each of us Brothers must carry out whatever tasks our Abbot gives us.'

I saw my chance to profit from his unhappiness.

'That's why you're staring so hard at the undug stink-trench eh Brother?' I sighed. 'If only staring would clear those filthy clumps away eh? Looks like the channel's blocked back to the main-midden.'

Before he could answer, I continued. 'Have no fear Brother, we'll clear your filth-ditch for you in no time. All we ask for in return is a bite to eat.'

'What?' cried Clodus.

'You don't want a blow-back,' I continued cheerily. 'Why, there's enough stew and slurry in there to fill a sea-king's sink-hole. You're lucky you've bumped into a master drain-maker and his er, trench-mate. Arnuf, fetch the tools from our ship.'

'Ship?' barked my bewildered companion.

'Yes ship!' I cried. 'Our roundship – where we keep the tools of the trade so we always stand ready to help strangers in need of our ditch-digging, trench-clearing and bog-draining skills.'

'What roundship?' asked Arnuf.

I hopped over and had a word in his ear.

'When I say "roundship" I mean the barrel we were washed up in. If we are to convince Brother Clumpus there, that we are master drain-makers, he will expect us to carry the tools of the trade.'

Slowly, the monk turned to face me.

'The pair of you are drain-makers, did you say?'

'Aye Brother. Master drain-makers, in fact.'

I barked at Arnuf to shift himself.

'On second thoughts Arnuf – forget the tools, just get down there and dig it out with your bare paws.'

Arnuf gazed mournfully at the muck-filled ditch.

'I have need of a bite to eat and a drink of mead. Brother – what say you that we stop for a quick mead break whilst Arnuf sniffs out the blockage?'

The monk looked as if all his prayers had been answered and climbed out whilst my trench-mate Arnuf took his place in the stinking ditch.

'Sit down here – or perhaps there – a little bit down wind of me,' I gasped.

Now I was ready to trick him out of his lunch.

'It is thirsty work Brother. Ah – I see my bottle is empty – alas. Let us drink your meat-mead instead.'

He sprang back, his hackles rising and wide-mouthed as a look of fear and disgust spread across his face.

'Meat-mead?' he spluttered, as if the words were fouler than drain-water.

His eyes flashed in anger and then he looked towards the sky and started pawing at the wooden cross-sticks at his collar.

'Meat-mead? It is the devil's own brew. I have sworn never to taste that dreadful drink!' declared the monk.

'What? No meat-mead?' gasped Arnuf.

'Not a single drop,' growled Brother Clodus.

'Not even on a feast day?' demanded Arnuf. 'Surely you must wet Wodin's whistle once a week?'

'Never!' cried the monk, shaking at the sound of this name.

'Not even on a Wodinsday?' asked Arnuf cheerily.

I thought it best to put a stop this chatter.

'Ignore my trench-mate Brother. He fell off a longboat when he was a pup. Now he can speak no sense at all and is prone to babble like a weak-wit.'

The monk's expression changed. Now he was full of concern for the poor fool standing next to me.

'Are you sick or hungry friend?' he asked. 'When strangers come to the monks of Sine Carne in need of food or drink, we always heal them and feed them.'

'For truth?' I asked in amazement.

'Aye! It is the law – laid down by The Thing.'

I clasped his paw and looked up to the sky.

'Feed strangers you say? Well now, there's a law that is very sensible and kind.'

'The Thing?' called Arnuf. 'That doesn't sound too good.'

I noticed Arnuf take something out of his pocket and rub it for good luck, so I snatched it out of his paw.

'Hey!' he cried. 'That's mine!'

He snapped at me and it fell into the mud. It was a tiny silver charm.

'Give that back!' he growled.

The monk looked at me with sad eyes.

'Return it to him, friend. Stealing what belongs to another dog is wrong,' he said.

'Well said. Thank you Brother,' said Arnuf.

Cursing under my breath, I did as the monk asked.

'Bless you!' he whispered, smiling at my kind act.

'What have you got there Arnuf?' I asked.

'That's my lucky hammer,' Arnuf explained. 'When I rub it, it protects me from evil.'

The Brother made a sound like a crow that's been bitten by a snake. Then he began to clutch at the cross-sticks on his collar. I growled at Arnuf to get digging.

'You were saying, about this Thing...' I began.

'Ah yes,' said the monk. 'The Thing comes around every month when the moon is full. It's coming today.'

Arnuf reached inside his pocket again.

My war-shy nerves began to rattle. Maybe my weak-witted friend was right to smell a rat? Not that he'd be able to smell anything near that fetid filth-drain.

'You mean this land is cursed? By a Thing?' I asked.

'No!' cried the monk. 'Well, I cannot lie. Yes, we are cursed. But not by the Thing...'

Well, the meak-minded monk did not have to mumble another word. I knew I'd been had! What kind of pack puts free food in the mouths of strays? Dark thoughts set sail across my mind. Free food? It was I, poor Beowuff who was to be the lunch – I was being fattened up for slaughter! I guessed that this horrible Thing came to the island and carried away warriors in its jaws. And the Brothers stood praying as it took its bloody tribute every night when the moon was full.

The birds twittered gently under golden sun.

Without another word, I ran off down the beach like a fox with a burning brush.

I have a coward's eye for a bolt hole. But there were no decent hiding places in sight – I saw nothing except endless stretches of cursed golden sand.

Then I spotted an island out in the bay. It was a long way off, but it was inhabited by the look of the tiny wooden buildings. Looking out towards the island, I noticed a narrow line of grey stepping stones.

'Thor's paws!' I cried. 'It's a causeway.'

It is said that causeways were thrown down by angry giants when the world was young. That would make sense. Giants are widely agreed to be lump-headed luggers with brains the size of chestnuts rattling around in their oversized brain-cases. Whoever designed the causeway was a fool. As a means of defending an island, a causeway it is about as useful as a straw cauldron! Attackers can sit sharpening their axes until the tide goes out, when they can trot up to the gates.

My dear old mother Mingingfrith loved to entertain us pups with her sagas of sorrowful happenings. One of her favourites was the tale of how a beautiful princess called Hallgerd Long-legs found herself stranded whilst crossing a causeway to Gnorway. I'll never forget mother's description of how poor Hallgerd howled as the cold sea rose past her shapely ankles to her royal snout. Mother said that she was too proud to swim. I do not know how such weak-wits manage to get themselves drowned, because it is plain as a pig-stick when it is safe to cross a causeway and when it is not. This one was safe – the sea-soaked stones were not yet dry – so I shot across and collapsed panting at the wooden gates.

'Let me in!' I wailed. 'Have pity! Do not bar the way to a poor stranger who needs to shelter behind your walls. I beg you, in the name of whatever is good in this world – will you not take pity and open the gate?'

'Give it a push,' called a voice. 'It's not locked.'

CHAPTER TWO

THE ORDER OF SINE CARNE

Heaving my weight against the gates, I pushed until I feared my gut-sack would burst. I strained in vain until the door swung open. Not daring to risk a glance behind me, unless the Thing was at my heels, I charged in and made for the building with the thickest walls. Not waiting to ask permission, I barged through a stone door into a packed chamber – full of monks – all babbling and chattering and muttering at once.

A high voice howled and the hall fell silent.

'But why my Brothers?' moaned a sad-faced hound. 'Why does He allow these hellish dragons to torture his loyal servants? It is too cruel!'

'Dragons?' I gasped. 'It's worse than I thought!'

'Oh my Brothers! What have we done to deserve this?' he howled again. 'We live pure and peaceful lives. We have given up eating meat and bones. What else is there for a good dog to do to please Him?'

Judging by their howls, the rest of the monks didn't have any answers to the monk's questions.

But a lone voice called out in a fearsome growl: 'Truly it has not happened by chance, but it is a sign that we have sinned. Somehow we have offended Him. And now, we who are left must stand up, fight bravely and defend His monastery.'

Fear rolled over me like a cartwheel over a jellyfish. When I hear talk of fighting, my gut-sack always begans to quiver. I was ready to turn-tail and flee when I spotted someone familiar coming in behind me. It was my weak-witted bench-mate Arnuf. He reeked of drains. The meatless diet of the monks didn't agree with the Brothers guts, judging by the stench. Arnuf clattered into the centre of the throng, panting and whimpering apologies to the monks.

'Whatever do you think you're doing?' barked a thundering voice.

Arnuf is so nervous that he gets worried watching sheep standing still in a field. He cowered at the growls of the bullying Brother, until a kindly old dog spoke.

'Brother Hardlarder. Have you forgotten our promise to help strangers? The doors of this monastery are always open. Who are you friend? What do you need?'

I needed no further encouragement. I pushed my way towards Arnuf and addressed the old hound.

'My apologies Brothers. I am named Beowuff and this is my companion Arnuf. We are poor travellers and we do not wish to disturb your meeting...'

When they heard these words, a gasp of shock rocked the room. It was followed by mumbled prayers.

'We do not use the word "meeting" explained the kindly old Abbot. 'For it is against our law to mention the forbidden flesh in this place. Instead our gathering is called The Thing.'

'Eh?' yapped Arnuf, turning his head sideways in wonder. A young voice at my side spoke in whisper.

'We Brothers can't say any word with "meat" in it. The word "meeting" sounds like "meat" – so we have to call it 'The Thing' instead.'

Arnuf gasped, stunned as a stoned crow.

'What? For truth? Never mind not eating meat? Now you can't even talk about it?'

'Aye – that is our law,' explained the young novice.

'How about "meat-plate"? Surely you can say that?'

'No!' cried the young novice, in horror.

'Arnuf!!!' I cried, clamping a paw around his snout.

'Forgive him,' I called. 'He'll go on spouting like a whale-fish unless I stick a cork in his blow-hole.'

But Arnuf snapped his snout free.

'Can you say meat-pie? demanded Arnuf.

'Arnuf! That's enough!' I cried.

The room seethed like an unwatched caldron. Some of the Brothers, (who'd lived sheltered lives), began to shout out prayers for our forgiveness. Others barked in anger that we'd spoken ungodly words and demanded that we should be turned out of their house.

The Abbot, their leader, was a wise old dog who spoke in a voice which was grave and calm.

'Enough! Take our visitors to the Uttery before the hour for food is past,' he ordered.

'Where are we off to?' asked Arnuf.

'Do ye not have ears? Follow me to the Uttery,' growled Brother Hardlarder, rising from his bench.

Arnuf looked puzzled.

The young novice, Fastwagger bounded over.

'He means the "Buttery", where we monks eat our meals,' he explained in a whisper.

Hardlarder overheard him.

'Hush! Don't say that sinful name!' he commanded.

'What name? Buttery?' asked Arnuf.

'Sssh!' whispered Fastwagger. We cannot say the 'B' word either.'

'You can't say "butter"? That's madness!'

'Silence!' commanded Hardlarder in a voice that would have stopped a charging bear.

He led us to another ancient hall. I was surprised to see that this one contained an enormous barrel.

'What's that?' asked Arnuf.

'That's Brewboiler,' whispered Fastwagger. 'It is the very latest thing in mead-brewing...'

'But you don't drink meat-mead,' interrupted Arnuf.

'We're brewing meatless mead,' said Fastwagger. 'You should try it. Once you've tasted our meatless mead, you'll never go back.'

But his dour senior soon put a stop to this talk.

'Stop your mindless chatter!' growled Hardlarder. 'Did you not know that He hears every word you say?'

As we trotted solemnly into the Uttery, the last monks were leaving. I snatched a biscuit from a plate.

'Put that back,' barked Brother Hardlarder.

'You slack-bellied strays – you expect the monastery to feed you. And how do you repay us? By stealing the food from our plates before we've said our prayers.'

'Sorry Brother,' I said choking on a mouthful of hard biscuit. 'These monk-biscuits are a little dry,' I spluttered. 'I don't suppose you've got something to wash them down with? A splash of mead perhaps?'

'Dry?' growled Hardlarder, foaming in fury. 'How dare you condemn my cooking. You ungrateful cur!'

'Brother Hardlarder is in charge of cooking our meals,' explained Fastwagger. 'He takes food seriously.'

'Apologies Brother,' I choked. 'I did not mean to 'condemn' your cook-craft...'

'Beggars cannot be choosers. You'll respect our laws or go to bed hungry,' warned Hardlarder.

The Abbot's friendly voice spoke next.

'Strangers often find our rules hard to understand. Brother Hardlarder – please can you feed our guests?'

'If it was up to me, they'd not get a crumb until they swore to abandon the sin of eating meat forever,' growled Hardlarder. He gave me the kind of disgusted look that a cat reserves for a brine-bath.

The Abbot smiled, humouring the old sour-snout.

'While I am Abbot, we will help strangers. Loving the poor brings us closer to the heart.'

Then Arnuf spoke.

'Are you allowed to say "heart" then?' he asked. 'Heart is a type of meat isn't it? Like liver?'

Shut your word-hole Arnuf!' I begged. 'Er – tell me good Abbot. When is dinner served?'

As these words left my mouth, a solemn bell began to toll. Its clanging chimes rose up to the roof. The last of the Brothers walked off in silence down the corridor.

'Hark! I fear you've missed it,' cried Brother Hardlarder. I swear I caught a little glee in the old monk's voice. 'Now you'll have to wait until we break our fast before we can feed you.'

'Break your fast?' gasped Arnuf. 'Can't you break your supper instead?'

'Our laws must be obeyed,' answered Hardlarder.

The meatless life hadn't made him a happier dog. I expect his tail had forgotten how to wag!

'Ignore him Brother – his brain-case was bashed when he was a pup,' I added.

'That, I can believe,' replied the sour-snout.

'What a terrible thing to befall a poor young whelp,' sighed the old Abbot.

I was hungry as a battlefield raven on a truce day. My sly eyes were searching for scraps, so I wasn't really thinking when the Abbot asked:

'How did that unhappy accident happen?'

'Er, in an ill-fated pig-sticking contest,' I replied.

'Pig-sticking!!' cried the old monk in horror, backing away from Arnuf as if he had the plague.

'Did I say pig-sticking? I meant pig-lifting,' I said, paddling my word-ship back upstream. 'Pig-lifting contests are common all over Gutland. They hold them as a warm-up to their annual wife-sniffing festivals.'

So Arnuf went to bed hungry that night. I was alright, for I'd sneaked back and stolen a bag of biscuits from the hall while the monks were praying, for me perhaps?

CHAPTER THREE

THE FURY OF THE NORTHPACK

What's this? Have some of you Carls drunk more meat-mead than your bladders can hold? You'd better get off to the leaking post quick and drain yourselves. Off you go! Fram! Fram! Fram!

While they have gone to 'water the great tree', I'll take this chance to talk to you Thanes, as you're the ones with the brains.

I expect some of you are wondering what was going on in the brain-case of old Beowuff. Why was I hanging around in this unhappy monk-hole when I had been told that a pack of war-dogs was on the loose? In truth, I'd decided to take to my heels and flee. But the thought of a warm bed and some monk-mead for breakfast was very appealing. Remember that I'd been starving in a barrel for the last three weeks. If I had known that the Brothers' attackers were Dragon raiders, I'd have fled from that unlucky monk-house like a rabbit from a pack of hunting hounds.

The good Brothers had fallen under a shadow from the North. These Dragons were the meanest pack of hack-happy hounds that ever pillaged a village. Did I not explain in my last saga about how the Half-Dragon had flayed one of King Ruffgar's ears off with a burning whip?

This lot were flint-hearted war-worms. They could

not fly or breath fire, but they left the lands of their victims in smoking ruins and they roamed the seven seas, looting and killing at will. These Dragons had sailed to their longboats up to the Brothers' happy island and 'blighted it', as the Skalds would say.

Not knowing of the danger, I dozed happily in my bed of straw. I slept without a care in the world, except for the grumbling noise coming from Arnuf's belly. It was loud enough to wake the ancestors from the sleep of ages. In the end I had to give him a stolen biscuit in order to get some peace and quiet. I was just nodding off again when I heard shouts at the door and a bell began to clang.

For a horrible moment I feared it was the monks raising the alarm. But I was greeted by a familiar voice.

'Wake! Master ditch-diggers! Get out of bed and follow me!'

'What?' I cried. 'Where are you going at this hour?'

'To the drains of course,' cried the voice. It was Brother Clodus. 'For the morn bell hath rung, we've said our prayers and now we must all get about our work.'

'Morn bell?' I moaned. 'But it's still dark as a death-mound outside.'

'It is three o' clock already masters,' said Clodus, licking Arnuf about the face to wake him. 'Brother Hardlarder told us to wake you at the first bell of the morning,' he said in a hushed voice, 'but some of the other Brothers thought you could do with a lie-in.'

'Hel's bed!!!' I cried. 'Leave me in peace, I pray!'

I pulled a pile of straw over my head and snuggled back down.

Then a voice at my side said:

'We should go with Brother Clodus – fair's fair.'

'Silence! You slack-witted sleep-stealer!' I cried. 'Will you give me no peace by day or night?'

'Beowuff,' said Arnuf seriously. 'We'd better help.'

'Oh?' I cried, poking my sleepy snout out of the straw-pile and rounding on the bothersome Brother. 'I see. It's like that, is it?'

'Like what?' asked Clodus.

'If we do not obey your commands, You'll turn us out of our beds and send us begging down the highway! We'll be alone in the night, at the mercy of the Dragon-pack.'

'No!' cried the monk in horror. 'That is not our way.'

'For truth?' I asked seriously.

'Stay and sleep if you do not want to join us at work.'

'Fine,' I laughed. 'Good night to you Brother!'

Sleep came quickly and I paid no heed to the noises of the Brothers as they went about their duties. Annoyingly, one of the them came and opened the door of my cell, for it was the rule that no monk could stay behind closed doors.

When I awoke for the second time, it was still dark outside – and the night was cold as the grave, without even a shroud of clouds. Bright stars leapt out of the skies like icy diamonds. I saw many constellations: the Wagon and the One-eyed Giant. It was so clear that the goat and the Bear and the Raven could all be seen.

I gazed in wonder at the silent beauty of the twinkling sky-diamonds. I was just dreaming of getting hold of a ladder big enough to climb up and steal them, when I heard a voice at my side.

'Beowuff? I must speak with you.'

'Not now!' I answered, 'Can't you see I'm busy?'

'That is what I must speak with you about,' said Fastwagger, for it was he who had come to my cell. 'Brother Hardlarder says that star-gazing is against our rules. For it puts us in mind of the sky-gods.'

'Hardlarder!' I moaned. 'That miserable monk would suck the joy from Happiness herself. Now tell me Brother, is that Bodin's Boat up there, that I see?'

On hearing this Fastwagger gasped and grabbed at the cross-sticks on his collar.

'Do not speak that name here! I beg you,' he howled.

'What? Not even Happiness?' I replied. 'Where's the harm in Happiness?'

'She is a valkyrie, isn't she?' whispered Fastwagger. 'The Abbot has forbidden any talk of them. He says that the old gods will lead us down to the terrible fire.'

I could do with a fire, for it was freezing in that damp cell but I had enough sense not to mention it.

'Beowuff,' he asked. 'You are a dog of the world who

has travelled far...' he began seriously.

Then the young novice spilled his guts to me about all that had happened at the Thing. Much had been said, but little had been decided – which makes it like most of the meetings I've ever attended. The Brothers could not decide what to do about the Dragon-pack.

Things were turning from bad to worse. The raiders had even started carrying off monks as well as gold. Fastwagger hoped that the Abbot would come up with plans for defending Sin Carne but instead the talk was all about the drains, and ways to enlarge the brew-house, and whether more prayers should be said and when. And all the while there was a ravening war-pack on the loose who could lay waste to the place at any moment. This last thought set my hackles up and I began to shake.

'Have no fear, for we are not in any immediate danger,' said Fastwagger.

'How can you tell?' I howled.

'The wind!' he cried, sniffing at the breeze. 'The raiders only attack when the wind comes from the North. Now it blows from the South. Smell it and see.'

I rose from my bed of straw and sniffed the air. The breeze was blowing from the South. But suddenly there was an enormous clap of thunder and a freezing gust blew right into the cell, sending the straw bedding flying.

'The wind has turned!' bayed Fastwagger, rolling his eyes towards the heavens. 'You must find your friend

Skaldi and seek shelter.'

'Skaldi? I howled. 'Who's that?'

'Your travelling companion. We must find him, for danger follows when the wind blows from the North.'

'Oh, you mean Arnuf? Don't worry about him – he loves danger. I'm sure he'll catch up with us. Where exactly did you say we were fleeing too?'

'Listen! I beg you! Sine Carne will soon be under siege by Dragon raiders. I pray your friend is a faster runner than me, or he'll be taken and made a slave.'

'Fear not – he is with Brother Clodus. Your god will protect them. Let us flee from this... holy place at once.

'Lead on!' I cried, wondering what it would take to stir him to move before we were trapped like rats in a barrel. But Fastwagger sat back on his haunches, still babbling nonsense about helping those in need. I nearly fell down a well when I realised he meant Arnuf.

'My heart tells me that you should seek your friend,' cried Fastwagger.

I would have run off without either of them, but I needed Fastwagger to guide me to a safe hiding place. Then I had an idea.

'Didn't your wise old leader, the Abbot say that He would not see his pups come to harm when the heathens attack?' I asked.

'Aye – he did say something like that,' replied Fastwagger. 'But we should still look out for your friend. They're a vicious pack of killers.'

I rose and dragged him by the collar, all the time moaning in my most monk-like manner:

'He will protect us, with his shield of justice and his self-swinging sword.'

'Er, I'm not sure that He has got a self-swinging sword actually...' said Fastwagger.

'Of course He has!' I bellowed. 'The Mighty Thor has a self-swinging sword. All the top gods are using them. Asgard is full of self-swinging weaponry these days.'

I paid no heed to the monk's protests, for by now we had reached a crossroads.

'Which way do we run?' I asked in a panic.

'Er, Beowuff,' began Fastwagger.

'Faster Fastwagger! Make haste,' I begged.

'We monks believe that ours is the only god worth worshipping. It would be wise not to speak the name of Bodin, or Thor or the Valkeries...'

'I know a wise old saying: "Flee first and ask questions later,"' I cried.

'Promise me Beowuff!' he cried. 'Swear that you will never talk of that heathen god-pack again. But now is not the right time for a lesson...'

'I swear,' I lied. 'Now lead us to a hiding place!'

'Thank you,' said Fastwagger, taking off like a hare.

'May the gods defend us. I mean, may He defend us!' I cried, running after him.

CHAPTER FOUR

THE DRAGON RAIDERS

That fool Fastwagger. If he had shut his word-hole and spared the speech-making, we would have been away over the causeway and safe. But like any dog who has just learnt a new trick, he could not resist the chance to put me right about the heathen gods. While Fastwagger was jabbering, the jaws of the trap were closing. On board his longboat, the Half-Dragon was whistling up his war-pack. Each one of his warriors was licking his axe, sharpening his spear and packing a extra loot sack, ready to be stuffed full of monk-geld.

Not knowing what kind of peril I was in, I ran towards the gate, screaming like a cut snake.

As I arrived, two Brothers were heaving the oak doors closed and getting ready to bar them. The Abbot, Goodoldboyson, trotted up to the gate-guards and set about giving them a stern tongue-lashing.

'Good for you Abbot,' I cried. 'Tell them to shift themselves, for the Dragon raiders are on the hunt.'

'No!' cried the Abbot. 'The gates of the house of the Lord should always stand open.'

Then the old fool told them unbar the doors. I have never seen anything like it.

'My pardon Brothers' I cried, and I knocked one of them into the mud, so eager was I to flee that place.

I'd come to the start of the causeway. If only I could

rush across before the raiders landed, I'd be able to hide in the forest till their wickedness was done. A forest is always the friend of the war-shy and the bolt-battle. An experienced lurker like me could find a thousand hiding-holes in the trees. Certain that I could make it, I took off along the slimy stones.

I was half way across when I saw it – rounding the headland at a fair clip. Never have I seen a sea-cutter like that. When the ship-builders asked how they should decorate their Lord's new craft, the Dragon Lord must have ordered: 'Make it dreadful to the eye!'

My gut-sack shook when I saw this craft and I began to quake like a cat-licker. Out of the mist loomed a dreadful figurehead: a snarling dragon cracking a bear's skull with its teeth as if it were a goose egg. Over the wall of shields, I got my first sight of that dreadful pack – each dog of them as fierce as the monsters from the fables.

I am not a fighting dog, but I have heard it said that a 'good big 'un' will always beat 'a good little 'un'.

Well, this dragon-pack were big 'uns alright. Stocky mastiffs and pugs who looked like they ate raw muscle for breakfast, lunch and supper. Their coats were shiny and their sharpened fangs gleamed like gull's eggs. Their arrow tips were already blazing – ready to put the monastery to the torch. And each dog of them had come a-raiding with one thought in his mind: to stuff his lootsack full to bulging with monk-gold and relics. And if they had to raise that old hag-queen Hel from her deadly bed and turn the sea red with monk-blood to do it, that was all the better. I never met a more torch-happy pack of pillagers stalking the seven seas.

In a blind panic I turned and fled back down the causeway. A pain stabbed through my paw and I nearly went into the whale-road for an early bath.

For a moment, I thought that one of their fire-darts had found its mark in my leg. I looked down in horror. In my haste, I'd stood on a barnacle and torn off one of my claws. There was no way I'd make it to the trees. Scrambling up, I dashed back towards the great gates of Sine Carne monastery. The air turned blue as I screamed the foulest of curses, which I will not now record.

I barked in terror, howling at the gate-guards to let me in. But I needn't have worried. The gates were unlocked – just as the Abbot had ordered.

When I entered, I found the Brothers crouching in the mud and chanting. I heard the cracked voice of the old Abbot rise above all others.

'From the fury of the Dragon Raiders – deliver us oh Lord!'

I was thinking about having a word with the Abbot, to see if he might be persuaded to make a personal appeal to Him on my behalf, when a shower of flaming arrows flew over the wall and fell in the courtyard. There was a great blast of a war-horn, and shouts of delight. The Dragons had discovered that the gate was open.

The raiding party tore through and sprang about the place, plundering at will and laying their thieving paws on whatever they liked.

I will not dwell on the details of this war-pack but trust me when I say that there is only one thing worse than a Dragon raider, and that is a Dragon raider with the scent of monk-geld up his nose. I have seen a few loot-happy death-packs in my time: the Hackerfolk for one or old King Ruffgar's Thanes for another. But when it came to thievery, these Dragon raiders took the dog biscuit and devoured it whole.

They ran amok, snarling at the monks to deliver them gold and relics, food and mead, and all the time the poor Brothers could do nothing to prevent them.

Most of the monks threw themselves into the dirt and whimpered. Perhaps it was their meat-free diet that make them so meek and mild? A few of them sat with their noses to the sky and howled down the heavens for Him to help them. But help did not arrive, only a great pack of heathens: three longboats full of them.

Hardlarder's thoughts were for the monk's precious relics and treasures.

'Hide it well my Brother,' he growled, passing a cloth bundle to one of the young monks. 'Has the devil struck you lame? Run and see to it now.'

My greedy eyes began to twinkle.

For although the Brothers swore that they'd given away all their treasure, I remembered the old saying: 'There is no such thing as a poor monk, or just one hornful of meat-mead.'

I have a nose for treasure and for looting and I

would bet my bench-mate's backside that the young monk was carrying a bundle of relics and was going to bury it somewhere safe, protecting it from the raiders no doubt. I decided to tag along behind and see if I might help to share his heavy burden.

He stopped short when he saw me, and he must have caught something in my eyes. Something the Brothers call 'sin'. For he fled back and squeaked to that sour-puss Brother Hardlarder. Soon I was getting a mouthful about the sin of 'jealousy'. I didn't quite catch the old monk's meaning but I certainly caught a good gob of his drool. He was in a foaming rage about robbers (me) being worse than the raiders, for I was an enemy within the walls.

I was almost pleased when another horn-blast from the raiders stopped his babbling like a choke-stone in the gullet and he ran off to find the Abbot.

Whilst Hardlarder had been haranguing me, I spotted Fastwagger in the thick of the fray. I called out to him and he bounded over.

'Why Beowuff? Why?' he cried. 'You are a dog of the world. Perhaps you can tell me?'

I shook my head sadly. 'Why have they come, do you mean?'

He nodded sadly.

'I do have experience with foul-hearted cut-bellies like these,' I said. 'Right now, you ought to be asking: "What?" instead of "Why?"'

'I do not understand you Beowuff,' sighed the

young monk.

'What have this death-pack come for?" I explained. 'Ask yourself that – then give it to them. And be quick about it before they tear you a new prayer-hole.'

'What do you mean?' asked Fastwagger.

'They must have come for something. Gold? Relics? Bones?'

'We are Meatless Monks. We don't eat bones,' said a rolling voice. It was Goodoldboyson, the Abbot.

'Then they must be after your treasure,' I sighed, faking sympathy.

The old Brother didn't seem worried that his monastery was under attack. However, his tone was firm.

'Hoarding 'treasure' is against our law, we have to give away all our possessions before we join.'

Whatever the Abbot said, I have never known a monastery that does not have gold and relics in good store. Why, the monks might sup from wooden bowls but inside their vaults I've seen cross-sticks as long as swords, dripping with rubies and precious stones. They also keep golden candle-sticks, bright as a furnace and fine robes covered in gold-link chain as long as Heimdall's bridge.

I was just thinking up a scheme where the monks could give away all their money – to me, when I heard a howl like a skewered boar.

'Help! They defile our garden!' cried a voice.

The Brothers had a garden in the courtyard where

they grew herbs for curing the sick.

Two Dragon raiders were using it as a leaking post.

'Friends! Mind where you leak! You are fouling the garden. There are good herbs growing,' cried Brother Sagus, an ancient hound who was the master of the herb garden.

That was a mistake. The first raider was a pug-nosed brute, built like a stone sluice-gate. He beckoned to his weasel thin mate and they trotted over.

'What's that prayer-sayer?' growled the weasly raider, licking something black off his spear point and pacing towards the shaking cleric.

'Hold fast!' said the pug, with a wicked gleam in his patched eye. He drew an object out of his loot-sack. The sight made me shiver in advance, for I cannot bear to see blood spilled. I did not care to watch pug-face beat the Brother's brains out with his club.

I decided it was time to stop lurking and sneak off when a smell came to my nostrils. A smell that I had not smelled for many weeks. Meat!

For it was not a club that the pug held in his paw but a huge bone. I drank in another whiff of the meaty smell and it set my juices going. Soon my belly was rolling like a longboat in a gale.

'That one looks a bit scrawny,' said the pug. 'He looks like he needs feeding up.'

He stuffed the knee-bone into his own jaws and bit down hard. You could hear the crack as it yielded up its creamy marrow to the raider's fangs.

'Here you are Brother,' said the pug with a wicked leer. 'Help yourself!'

'No! I cannot,' said the Brother shaking his head.

'Go on! Have a little lick, it'll make you strong,' laughed the pug.

'It might even help grow you a backbone,' said his mate as he pushed the dripping bone-shard into the old monk's mouth.

'No!' cried the Brother in terror. 'It is forbidden. No meat can pass my lips!'

The weasel held his jaws open whilst the pug forced the bone into the poor monk's mouth.

'Forgive them,' said the Abbot, who was watching this happen.

'You cannot stay here Abbot,' said Fastwagger. 'It is too dangerous. We must get you to the inner sanctum where we can keep you safe.'

I liked the sound of that. Given the choice between running into the jaws of danger and lurking out of harm's way with the possibility of a little loot-picking, I will go a-lurking every time.

But the head howler himself was reluctant to leave. Thank the Bearded Bonefather that Fastwagger persuaded the Abbot to leave. I am not sure what he said exactly but it was something about saving the chronicles. At last, the old one agreed and so I trotted after the pair of them.

We went as fast as the old Abbot's feeble legs could manage. Over the stone flags, through an archway and off down a passage which ended in a stout oak door, as the sagas always put it. What other type of oak door is there?

Inside, the drafty room was lit by lines of candles. This was a surprise, since it was full of rows of precious chronicles. If I had a chronicle house, a store of sacred knowledge in priceless volumes, I would not have lit it with flaming wicks.

On a low bench before me, a Brother was copying a line of monk-runes from one book into another. Pictures leapt off the pages in floating colours: violets and reds and golds, glowing like wildflowers in the autumn corn.

I let out a loud sigh. The Abbot gave me a searching look, as if to say: 'Well, there must be something good in you after all, Beowuff, my old pew-mate.'

Now you might be surprised to find old Beowuffer moved by the sight of a row of runes in a monk-book. In fact, my eyes had caught sight of the clasp that held the book open. It was made of solid gold.

Just then, there came a thumping thud and the door swayed as the heavy axes of the raiders began to pound into it. The door looked like cheap Swedish pine. Here's a piece of advice – if you ever build yourself a bolt-hole, be sure to use decent Gnawegian wood.

'Break out the weapons Brothers,' I cried, backing away into the corner.

The Abbot shook his head, smiling sadly.

'We of the Sine Carne order are peace-loving monks. We have sworn not to harm other creatures.'

'Not even if the creatures are about to rip your ears off and feed them to your friends?' I asked.

The thumping grew louder. There were only moments left before the goddess Hel unleashed her pack.

The Abbot raised a paw to silence me.

'We must bear their taunts. These raiders must have been sent to us for a good reason.'

The young novice Fastwagger spoke up.

'Beowuff is right Abbot. We must fight back! They are evil. They commit new outrages with each attack.'

'Have a care Brother Fastwagger!' warned Hardlarder. 'Have a care! Remember the vow you swore to live in peace.'

'But...' began the young monk

The old Abbot shook his head.

'I fear that we must bear it. May He give us the strength to endure.'

As these words left his maw, there was a tremendous crack like a thunderbolt. The monks gazed up to the skies as if their cross-god had come down from the sky, but it was just the Dragon pack, punching their way through the door.

The first of the Dragons to step through was a Thane, by the look of him. He had a long sword with a notched blade and a mail coat on him. He didn't need these of course. The monks were about us much use in battle as a straw broadsword.

The Thane barked twice and three raiders sprang after him, drooling. They were all big brutes but their captain was the biggest. His name was Fangar.

He strutted over to where the monk was sat copying and snatched up the chronicle from the desk.

'Careful! I beg you!' whimpered the terrified Brother, shuddering as Fangar's paws touched the book.

His orange eyes searched the room and settled on a candle which was burning low in its metal holder. The light danced as Fangar held the book over the flame.

'Don't burn that chronicle! It is beyond price,' gasped the monk. 'It took me seven years to copy.'

'You'd better get scribbling again then,' laughed Fanger, as the smell of burning hide filled the room.

The raiders laughed and drew their daggers. This sort of dog comes armed with a choice of weapons when he goes loot-picking.

'May He protect us!' muttered the Abbot, clutching at the cross-sticks at his collar.

Fangar laughed. It was not the sort of pleasant laugh that you laugh when you hear that your king's wife has just run off with a Swede.

'Where was your cross-god when the mighty Thor sent the storm that blew us to your gates? Where was he then? Do not tell me he did not see it, for he sees everything. Was he scared to show his face?'

I was just thinking that Fangar might have had a point when Hardlarder came running over.

'Blasphemy!' he growled, squaring up to the Dragon raider, although the Thane was three times his size.

'What?' laughed Fangar.

'Blasphemy!' growled Hardlarder again. 'May He bite you down for what you have just said.'

That's done it, I thought, fully expecting Fangar to cut the talk short with a hack of the broadsword.

I have some experience with war dogs like these Dragon raiders. And when they are on a looting spree it is best to give over your bones and treasure, and keep your mouth shut.

Luckily, one of the other Dragons spotted the books on the table and seized one in his jaws.

'No!' cried a monk. 'Not the Chronicles of Fidus!'

He let out a yelp, as if the raider had seized hold of his own tail.

There was a horrid ripping as he tore the chronicle away from its golden clasp.

'This will make a pretty nose ring for my wife,' said the raider, leering at the gleaming gold. 'Sorry lads but it takes sleigh-loads of jewellery to keep her sweet.'

The others laughed. But Fangar let out a growl.

'Leave that! Remember the words of the Half-Dragon. Search everywhere for it!'

Now mark this well, all you good Thanes and Carls. 'Search everywhere for it!' said the raider. This is the sort of precious word-scrap that you hear in the sagas. The Skald telling the saga will try to sneak it in without you noticing it. Without fail, it will prove important. The rest of the tale is sure to hang upon it, like a monk-pelt on a raider's spear. What was Fangar searching for? I will not say just yet, but keep your ears open!

I heard Fangar's words at the time, but I paid no attention, for I was cowering like a cat-licker.

When they heard their Lord's command the war-pack sprang into action. The general effect was the sort of chaos you'd get when you set a bag of well-starved ferrets loose in a rabbit warren.

There were monks grovelling, raiders growling, the Abbot howling, Hardlarder praying, and priceless chronicles flying everywhere. And at the heart of this page-storm was your old bench-mate Beowuffer, looking for a chance to flee.

I found myself stood next to Fastwagger. The young Brother had his nose downcast, after his suggestion of a fight back had been slapped down by the others. Their Abbot had been quite right of course. Fastwagger stood as much chance against the Dragons as a kitten stands against a ravening wolf-pack.

Then I spotted a my chance to flee, so my worm-tongue wriggled into action.

'Brother Fastwagger,' I asked. 'Is there another way out of this room?'

'Why Beowuff? Are you going run off and leave us?' said a cold voice. It was that bitter-witted scorn-pourer Hardlarder. He had overheard me.

'Er, of course not. I was just saying to the Brother here that someone should go and fetch help.'

The sour-face shook his head and bared his teeth.

'Help? Really?' he laughed. 'Well there is no help for three hundred miles. That's why we must trust to Him.'

I turned away, sniffing the stonework at the back of the far wall. I felt a draught. The floor was made of earth, so I began to dig.

'What are you doing?' asked a kind voice. It was Fastwagger.

In fact, I was planning to dig a hole, and bury myself in it. But before I could answer, he interrupted.

'Ah!' he said. 'You're digging a tunnel aren't you?'

I nodded guiltily.

'I understand what you are doing!' he went on. 'You're trying to fetch Skaldi, aren't you?'

'Yes,' I lied.

By Skaldi, he meant my weak-witted bench-mate Arnuf. I hadn't seen Arnuf since he went drain-digging with Brother Clodus. He's about as 'comfortable in battle' as a meatless-monk at a blood-month feast. But for some reason, Fastwagger was sure that 'Skaldi' was the war-dog to save his bacon – or perhaps not – on account of the monks being meat-free.

The thought of Arnuf trotting to our rescue in battle would have made me sick if it wasn't so ridiculous. 'Help me! Two sets of paws can dig faster than one. Speed me on my way!'

A strange light came into Fastwagger's eyes.

'Follow me Beowuff' he cried. 'For I know another way out of here, which is both swift and secret.'

Well, I could have choked the young prayer-prattler right there and then! If he knew of another way out, why in the name of Thor's thunder did he not tell me about it earlier?

CHAPTER FIVE

DEEP DIGGINGS

astwagger scrabbled about around the base of the wall, mumbling pleas about being saved from the heathen's axe. While he was busy, I risked a look about the place. Some of the more enterprising Dragons had bound the Brothers up in fetters and were setting about the work of questioning them, using one of the heavier chronicles – I think it was Fidus – for encouragement. I could not see Hardlarder being questioned but I hoped they'd got that pious old sour snout. He deserved a good 'chronicling' after the way he'd treated me.

The rest of the Dragon pack were throwing chronicles everywhere and sniffing around for whatever they'd come for. Monk-geld most likely.

I almost laid an egg when I heard Fangar's command to 'Search every corner!' But at that moment, Fastwagger let out a yelp of delight and I span around. I saw that he had levered up a flagstone. Now every monk-hole has a tunnel, as sure as every pine tree has a nest. And this one was as musty as a drowned stag in a sinkhole. Some dogs love a ripe-rotten tang but I held my nose as I crawled into the hole and shut the trapdoor behind me.

It was cold as an Icelander's grave in those diggings. It was damp too. I shivered and pulled my cloak tight around me and began to crawl behind Fastwagger.

He was still muttering prayers to his maker and for once I would have joined in with him, if only I knew the words. My back legs were shaking and my thoughts were always on the Dragon pack. They might sniff out our bolt-hole at any time.

After a long crawl, I thought it safe to risk a rest so I called to Fastwagger to stop. Although he was just ahead of me, his shape was lost in the gloom. It was blacker than a troll's hankie down that pit.

'How far is there to go?' I called.

'I do not know,' came the reply.

'Thor's bolts!' I cried, fearing that the muddle-minded monk was leading me down a dead end.

'What do you mean, you don't know!' I snapped.

'I'm not sure where this tunnel leads,' explained Fastwagger. 'I've never followed it to its end.'

'You Brothers have no curiosity,' I muttered.

'I hope it will lead us to the beach,' he added.

I muttered a few choice word-scraps to myself, wondering if Fastwagger's meat-free diet had shrivelled his wits. Then I asked the obvious question:

'Tell me Brother. How can this tunnel possibly lead to the beach? This monk-house is surrounded by the sea, is it not?'

But I was wrong. He explained that Diggus, the monk who founded the monastery, was a master tunnel digger who had worked for the King of the Swedes, excavating all manner of underground dungeons.

'What? You expect me to believe that a dungeon maker gives up his job and to become the Abbot of a meatless monastery?'

'He wasn't always the Abbot. He was a mendicant first,' said Fastwagger.

'What by Bodin's Blind eye is a mendicant?' I growled, weary of all this mixed up monkery.

'A wandering monk,' explained Fastwagger. 'But before that he was a great builder. His tunnels could run under the ground or below the sea.'

I sniffed the damp air and listened, daring to hope that Fastwagger was right. Were there waves above our backs even now? Could we really make it to the safety of the beach? Oh happy thought!

We walked faster, and now I was dreaming of freedom. A quick dart across the sand and then I could disappear into the wild forest. If I never saw another monk again, it would be too soon.

With every pace, the darkness lifted and the air became fresher. Then a familiar sound came to my ears. It was the swishing of the breakers on the whale-road. Pushing past him, I stuck my nose out of the tunnel.

'Waves!' I cried, wagging my tail in joy and delight. 'You beautiful Brother! You marvellous monk!' I cried, licking his face. 'You've led me to freedom!'

But my hope soon broke like a white-capped roller.

The tunnel had come out half way along the causeway. Worse still, we were now in plain view of the Dragons. Three of their ships were at anchor.

'Meak-minded monks!' I cried, 'Why didn't that dolt Diggus finish the job? What kind of clueless-cleric digs half an escape tunnel?'

Fastwagger begged me to keep silent. For just a few tail lengths above us, the horde of happy hackers were busy carting their booty to their longboats. I say 'booty' but they'd stolen some strange loot. One of them was carrying a huge wooden table, one had an oak pew and the last pair were manoeuvring what looked like an enormous kettle.

'What have they got there?' I whispered.

'The thieving heathens!' said Fastwagger. 'They're making off with our mead-kettle!'

Every dog has something close to his heart and for this monk it was that old kettle, which he'd named Brewboiler. Fastwagger was learning the ancient art of brewing mead from honey and spring water. The monks mead was meatless, but it was very tasty.

'We must save Brewboiler!' cried the monk.

I was more worried about saving something close to my heart: my own skin. Already my mind had turned to the problem of how to make it past those loathsome longboats to the freedom of the beach.

Being a shameless bolt-battle has made me a master of pale-livered sneakery. The day was darkening early and the sea was as black as a coal-pit. The Dragon pack had their minds on looting. They were not looking for us. Perhaps we could slip past them unseen?

No! Even for a Lord of lurking like me it was too risky. Each boat had look-outs. If they spotted us it would end with an arrow through the throat.

As these thoughts were drifting through my mind, Brother Fastwagger thrust a bundle into my paws. I unwrapped it to find a long dagger and a helmet made of iron. 'Weapons!' I cried. 'Where by Loki's ears did you get those war-irons from?'

'They were hidden in the tunnel,' replied Fastwagger. 'Look, I have another.'

I ran my paw down the blade. It was blackened and notched, but as sharp as a shark's tooth.

Just then, I heard noises behind us.

'The Dragons!' I howled. 'They are upon us!'

I jumped back, putting the monk in between me and the enemy. But I was caught between the cruel sea and the Dragon-pack racing up the tunnel.

'May He forgive me for what I am about to do!' said Brother Fastwagger, raising his dagger and trying a few practice swipes. It was a sorry display of sword skills. He was waggling the blade through the air as if he was tempting a donkey with a carrot. My only hope was to sneak off whilst Fangar and his throat-cleaving crew were laughing at the sight of him.

The noises grew louder as we peered into the dark tunnel.

'Can you see anything?' I whispered.

Faster than the flap of a crow's wing, two hooded shapes flew from the mouth of the passage. The first was so surprised to see us that he slipped on the wet rocks and slid straight past my nose.

There was a loud splash.

'That'll serve you!' I muttered, smiling as he thrashed about in the freezing sea.

'Skaldi!' cried Fastwagger.

The 'raider' was none other than my weak-witted bench-mate Arnuf. He flailed about, spluttering and blowing salt-bubbles and calling for help.

'Help him!' cried Fastwagger in a panic.

'I don't know if he can swim,' I said, hoping that Arnuf would sink below the waves before the Dragons heard him spluttering.

Fastwagger and another figure, who had been running up behind Arnuf, dashed to the edge. They hauled my bench-mate out of the water. He struggled up, flapping like a speared flat-fish.

'Brother Clodus?' gasped Fastwagger. 'I give thanks that you've escaped from the heathen's axe.'

'Beowuff!' said Arnuf. 'Thank Thor you are safe!'

I thought that the monks might throw him back for this remark but they simply clutched at their cross-sticks and mumbled, the way they always did if the names of the old gods were spoken. It wounded them just to hear the name of Thor or Bodin.

'If I live to see another sunrise, it will be no thanks to you Arnuf,' I growled. 'Now shut your silly snout-hole and stop shaking out your coat. You've already made enough noise to rouse Hel from her death-bed. If the Dragon raiders capture us now, you and your mud-thumping monk-friend will be the cause of it!'

As Fastwagger greeted Clodus, I sat slack-jawed at the sight of Arnuf. There he stood, dripping sea-brine with a silly grin on his face as usual.

As Fastwagger reached the end of his tale, he explained his plan to fight through to the beach.

'May I be forgiven for what I am about to do?' muttered Fastwagger, taking out his dagger again.

By rights he ought to have been asking the war-god, for forgiveness. I am a fearful fighter, but even I know which end of a sword to point at the enemy.

Fastwagger grew serious.

'I have another blade Clodus. Are you with me?'

The other monk took hold of the sword for a moment, but then he dropped it as if it were a poisonous snake. He began to howl, then he shook his head and muttered, biting on the cross-sticks at his collar.

'What's wrong with him?' asked Arnuf.

'He wants to help. But we have sworn a vow not to fight,' explained Fastwagger.

'Come to think of it, so have I,' I announced.

Why should you have to be a monk to get yourself out of fighting? What about bolt-battle dogs like me? Well, two could play that war-shy game.

'For truth?' said Fastwagger, in surprise. 'Are you really a monk in disguise Beowuff?'

I nodded.

'Beowuff ...' began Arnuf, 'if you're a monk, how come you eat so much meat?'

'Because I'm fasting,' I answered. 'I'm on a special meat fast.'

I turned to the monks.

'Now listen Brothers. My bench-mate Arnuf, (who you Brothers call 'Skaldi') over there, is the only one of us who hasn't sworn any vows about not fighting. So he could… No. No I cannot ask it.'

'Ask what?' asked Fastwagger.

'No! Forget that I even mentioned it. It would be too noble,' I blathered.

'What can't you ask?' barked Clodus.

'What? What should I do?' asked Arnuf, at long last.

'Listen old friend,' I began in my kindest tone, 'If you run over and distract the Dragon raiders, we monks could slip past and make it to the beach.'

Arnuf twisted his head to the side, deep in thought.

'But no, it would be too selfless, too noble! Too much to ask…' I pleaded.

I waited for an age until at last, he answered.

'Alright, I'll do it!' said Arnuf.

'No! Skaldi! You cannot!' said Fastwagger.

'Yes I can,' said the noble idiot. 'Monks are not allowed to fight. It is the only way to save you.'

I don't know what had come over Arnuf but I decided to send him off quickly, before he turned war-shy.

'See the guards standing by that watch fire?' I whispered, pointing towards the Dragon's boat.

Arnuf nodded.

'Go and distract them. We'll escape.'

Without another word, Arnuf leapt up and took off down the causeway like a mad march hare.

'Come back!' I cried. 'You're going the wrong way!

If wits are water, there's a hole in Arnuf's bucket. He was born with less sense than Gorm the Gormless. He was running back towards the monastery.

'Stop!' I cried. 'You'll get us all slaughtered!'

The guards were so busy dividing their loot that they didn't spot him. I sat in silence with the two monks. Neither of them looked as if they could be as easily persuaded as Arnuf. There was nothing for it. I'd have to wait it out. We'd be safer back in the tunnel.

Then I felt it – a wave washing over the lip of our hollow. The tide was on the turn. Soon the white stones of the causeway would be covered by the whale road. I sprang back into the tunnel and felt another freezing wave run over my paws. There was no way back either. Our hiding place would soon be under the waves.

'What do we do now?' I whined.

'We pray,' said Clodus. 'Will you lead us in the prayers Brother?'

After a while I realised that he was talking to me.

'Er, I'd love to, but...' I began.

'Look!' said Fastwagger. 'Ships!'

The first of the three longboats had slipped its anchor and was headed away. I shivered like a captured Dane on a Swedish leash. We watched the water level rise in the passage, willing the ships to sail away. It would come down to a matter of minutes. What cruel luck to be drowned in this soak-hole just as the enemy were leaving. But the Dragon captains were keen to catch the tide and although they were a pack of cut-throats, their crews knew how to handle a boat.

So the three monks, Brother Fastwagger, Brother Clodus and Brother Beowuff rose from their watery pit and scrambled back down the causeway to Sin Carne.

CHAPTER SIX

HELP FROM HEROES

When we returned, it looked as if an angry storm had blown through the monastery. I suppose, in a way it had.

The monks kept to their routines and went amongst the wounded, giving out their herbs of healing. Not that a pawful of monk-weeds is much use if you've got a Dragon raider's axe wedged in your brain-case.

They called a Thing to discuss what was to be done. A council of peace, as the Abbot put it.

The monks had lost none of their love of rules and bells. I came late to the Thing and was still wiping the crumbs from my maw as I took my place and sat down where their great table had once stood. For the Dragon raiders had stolen everything that wasn't nailed down.

Brother Clodus spoke first.

'It is no use,' he cried. 'We are helpless against the heathens.'

'May I share my thoughts?' asked Fastwagger.

The Abbot nodded.

'I know that it is a sin to say it. But if only we had amongst us some war-dogs – who could help us.'

Have you guessed what he meant? The pleading idiot was looking at me to deliver him. I fear that he had not believed me when I'd told him I was a monk!

'Yes,' I said sadly. If only you did... that would be

a great blessing.'

If this pitiful prayer-pack thought I'd be any use against the Dragon Raiders they must be as mad as mink in the mating season.

I tried to ignore them, but the whole hall just sat there in silence waiting for my word.

'We have prayed all night for help,' said Clodus.

'Will you help us Brother Beowuff?' asked Fastwagger.

I had no choice but to answer.

'Yes...' I replied.

When they heard me, the monks began to cheer and shout 'Thank goodness! Our prayers are answered!'

Well I wasn't going to be caught like that.

'I'll help you with the praying,' I said earnestly.

Stick that in your prayer-holes and choke on it, I thought. Old Beowuffer would pray to their god and all of the others as well, if it would do any good.

'You misunderstand me Brother Beowuff,' said Fasterwagger. 'We know that you are a monk, but we were hoping for a different kind of help. A more practical type of assistance.'

Then I heard a familiar voice calling from the back of the hall.

'Say no more Brother. We'll help!'

It was my muddle-minded bench-mate Arnuf. That brave dash in the wrong direction must have turned his wits to mush. Now he was strutting about the hall like a hero from the sagas. The monks howled in excitement but I liked him more when he was war-shy.

The Brothers let out another cheer and banged upon the floor where they sat. The raiders had stolen their benches and now they had to sit on the cold stones.

My heart sank like a scuttled sea-cutter.

That dunder-brained Arnuf was about to get both of us skewered.

'I am sorry Brothers, but it will take more than just one, or even two heroes to take on a whole pack of Dragon raiders. Surely you can see that?'

Now it was the Abbot's turn to speak.

'Go and fetch more 'heroes' for us,' he begged. 'You know the ways of war. We meatless monks have no understanding of things like that. Here in the Sin Carne order we are dogs of peace,' he said.

'Will you do this for us?' pleaded Fastwagger.

'Er...' I began. But before I could wriggle out of it, my heroic bench-mate jumped in.

'We'll do it! We'll save Sin Carne. We swear!'

'No! He unswears it,' I protested. 'See! He had his paws crossed when he made that promise.'

'I did not,' said Arnuf.

'Let us give thanks,' muttered the Abbot.

Arnuf looked ever so pleased with himself, thinking that the monks were thanking him.

As this went on I racked my brain for a likely excuse to get me out of this peril. The well-meaning monk-pack was about to place me in deadly danger. But before I could spin them another yarn, old Hardlarder piped up. I was sad to see that he still had all four paws intact. It was a shame Fangar hadn't sliced his sour snout off back in the chronicle room.

'How much gold and mead will you need to hire the heroes?' he asked.

I could hardly believe my ears.

'Gold and mead did you say?' I said in amazement.

'Aye – how much? We have both,' said Hardlarder.

'In good store,' added Fastwagger.

The old sour-puss shot him a look that would have stopped a wild-wolf in its snow-tracks. Then he put his paw to his lips and made the sign of silence.

'Hold on,' I said. 'I thought you monks have vowed to give up gold – not to mention the meat-mead.'

'How dare you!' growled Hardlarder in a fury.

'Our mead is meat-free,' reminded Fastwagger.

Well bench-mates, I sat there and I tried not to smile. I knew it! I have never met a monk yet who did not have some gold or silver relics stashed away somewhere. They probably had a bone-hoard too which they passed around secretly at midnight.

Then the Abbot whispered:

'Beowuff. If the Dragon raiders ever were to learn about our gold, they would raise this place to the ground, and kill every monk in Sine Carne monastery.'

'Your secret is safe with me father. I swear it,' I replied. For once I was not lying. I had no intention of blabbing to the dragon-pack. I wanted to get my own paws on the monk's gold, I didn't want to fight Fangar and his mates for it.

'Brother Hardlarder,' ordered the Abbot. 'Go to the place we do not speak of and fetch the thing that cannot be named – in a bag.'

'You might need a sack – I'll need plenty of the thing that cannot be named,' I called.

Brother Hardlarder gave me nasty look. Then he went away muttering something under his breath. I fancy that he was not praying.

As Hardlarder was leaving, the old Abbot rang a bell, the signal for the end of The Thing. But he asked Arnuf and I to stay.

Some time later, Hardlarder came back with a sack and emptied it out onto the floor. There were jewels, gold and silver chains and coins from faraway lands. Some with writing like the thinnest stalks of waving corn. I cared little for the craft of the goldsmith as it all melts down the same. As well as this there were drinking horns, brooches and a good quantity of silver.

I tried not to leap for joy.

'Put all the gold into a big pile so that I can inspect it,' I cried. 'And bring me some mead and biscuits too!'

'How many heroes can you get for this?' asked the Abbot in seriousness.

'For all that gold? A whole host of them!' said Arnuf. He had never seen so much loot in all his life, and neither had I, if truth be told. But I held my nerve, in case the monks were holding back the good stuff.

'Hmmm... Not as many as you used to. Battle-trained war-dogs don't come cheap you know.'

'How many?' growled Hardlarder.

'Ooh... er, three or four I expect,' I said calmly.

'Surely more than that?' shouted the sour-snout in a rage. 'That gold-heap would ransom a king. You can hire fifty swords for that much.'

I looked at Hardlarder in amazement.

'For a monk you're very knowledgeable about the price of hiring war-dogs and mercenaries,' I muttered.

The old Abbot spoke next, after looking around to make sure that no one could overhear him.

'Brother Hardlarder was a mercenary himself – before he joined the order,' he confessed.

I did not doubt his word. That old hirling Hardlarder was to prove a thorn in my paw, I wanted to leave with all the gold, and I would have convinced the Abbot to send me off with a cartload of treasure. But Hardlarder spoke against this plan.

'It's too dangerous,' he tutted. 'Come back with the warriors, and we will pay them when the task is done.'

Thinking fast, I gave him the best answer that sprang to my gold-dazzled mind.

'I'll need a few sacks full of treasure at least – just to show the heroes that I am in earnest,' I said.

'When are we leaving?' asked a voice at my side.

I had forgotten my newly heroic bench-mate Arnuf.

I thought about a reason why he should stay to guard the monastery but a growl from Hardlarder showed that he wasn't going to let me leave alone.

'Soon old friend,' I replied.

'Can we take some biscuits and meat-mead?' asked Arnuf.

Hardlarder scowled at this, but let it pass.

'Meatless mead,' reminded the Abbot. 'In fact, if you were to swear to give up meat eating while you are on our quest, that would be even better.'

Arnuf wagged his tail – although I could tell that he had no clue what the Abbot was asking him to do.

'Who knows what dangers the road will bring,' mused the new hero of Sin Carne.

The next morning, the monk-pack marched out and crossed the causeway to wave us off.

The Brothers loaded us up with enough food and mead for a two-week walk. After a long discussion, they gave me two small bags of gold.

I was eager to take to the road but there was another delay whilst Fastwagger hung cross-sticks around our collars, muttering in his usual manner. I found it unpleasant but Arnuf seemed touched by this present and I thought I saw a tear in his eye.

I strained my eyes to look out across the sea. It was jewell blue, glowing like the pictures in the monks' chronicles. My guts twisted in fear. For a horrible moment, I thought I'd caught sight of a mast on the horizon. I tugged at Arnuf's collar.

'Wait!' he called. 'Where can we find heroes for hire?'

Hardlarder gave me another look, as if to say: 'Why the devil haven't you asked about this before?'

'There is a settlement five days walk from here. If there are heroes for hire that is where they'll dwell,' said Fastwagger.

'May your road be blessed,' said the old Abbot.

Fastwagger leaned close and whispered his advice.

'Mind you do not stray and take the road for the mountains...' he said with a shiver.

'Goodbye,' I said, glancing at the sea. The ocean looked far too blue to be true.

'For up in the mountains, the Outdwellers... dwell.' said Fastwagger.

'Outdwellers? What are they doing, dwelling out there?' asked my heroic friend.

'It is said,' whispered Fastwagger. 'That unnatural pups who have been cast out – roam the stony hills to the east, and feast on unwary...'

'Farewell!' I cried, not wanting to stand around listening to a monk prattling on when the Dragon-pack could sail back and slay me at any moment.

'It is said that bad ghosts walk those nameless tracks,' said the young monk with a shiver.

Well, on any ordinary Freya's day or Thor's day this manner of talk would have set Arnuf howling, quivering and leaking buckets. But today he just clutched at the new cross-sticks on his collar and smiled at Fastwagger as if no foul fiend could frighten him.

'Fear not Brothers,' he said coolly. 'We'll bring back your heroes.'

CHAPTER SEVEN

SNOW WORRIES

When I was sure we could not be spotted from the monastery, I started to look for a suitable cross-roads. It wasn't long before I found it. Without delay, I turned off the road and up a stone-strewn track towards the hills.

Three miles later, Arnuf cried:

'Hold! Beowuff, I have the feeling that we're going the wrong way.'

I ignored him and carried on walking.

Unfortunately, he would not shut up.

'Beowuff,' he said seriously. 'Remember what the old Monk-father said. We must make for the settlement. That's where we'll find heroes.'

I stopped in my tracks.

'Heroes?' I cried. 'Have you lost your wits? Do you think I would willingly take up with a pack of loot-mad glory hounds?'

'But...' he spluttered. 'We're doing it for the monks.'

'I'd rather throw myself to the Dragon-raiders,' I snapped.

'But how are we going to save the monastery from Fangar and his Dragon-pack, without heroes to help us?' he sniffed.

'We're not,' I said flatly.

It felt better out than in.

'Beowuff,' he growled. 'You took the Monk-father's gold coins. You promised... You said...'

My next words felled him.

'I promised that I would 'find' heroes. I never said I'd do any of the saving myself.'

'Well,' he whined. 'We won't find any heroes if we go this way. It's the road to the mountains, where the Outdwellers live. We don't want to be going up there.'

Now at this point, my poor brain was caught by a two-horned problem. Here was old Beowuff, clean away down the road, with a couple of bags of monk-geld. Could I be happy and lie in bed content with two treasure-bags? Alas – no. For try as I might, I could not banish the thought of the treasure of Sine Carne from my brain-case. I was geld-struck.

However, maybe the Dragon raiders knew about the monk-gold too? Is that what Fangar had meant when he'd told his pack: 'Search for it!'

Then we came to the matter of heroes. If we found sword-dogs for the Abbot, then old Beowuff could forget about getting his paws on the monks' gold-pile. The noble hirelings would kill us first, then take the lion's share of the loot, or both. Or perhaps the Dragons would come back and leave our hired heroes sleeping in a death-mound, with poor Beowuff lying next to them with an arrow in his eye. To put it plainly, my heart was for thieving, but my legs were for leaving.

Then I remembered the words of my dear old mother Mingingfrith:

When you have a problem,
and you cannot WORK it out,
Pick up your heels and WALK it out.

A good long walk was her answer to everything. I remember her saying the exact same thing to my Uncle Deerwuff. He followed her advice and walked straight off an ice-cliff. But that apart, a long walk is ever the friend of the thinker. So for now, I was content to tramp onwards whilst I worked out how best to place my thieving paws on the rest of the monk-gold.

The track took us on and as the day passed, the mellow countryside gave way to a grimmer landscape of strangled woods and drowned fields.

Do any of you Thanes need to pay a visit to the 'yellow bush'? If you do, now is a good time to go, while I tell of that strange and stragglesome land.

Broken oaks stood choked on dour moors.

Ravens flew over lines of pines and a withering wind from the North blew shivers down the spines of the grim hills. Drizzle blasted over drowned heaths. I came across a rune-stone but a hundred gales had worn its writing smooth beyond understanding.

Ah? You Thanes are back again. Good! I will spare you the rest of the dull detail.

It was hard walking and before long I had worked up a thirst and was cracking into the flask of mead that the Brothers had packed for us.

'Got any more of those monk-biscuits? I asked.

'Throw me over your pack, for I know Fastwagger has stashed them in there somewhere.'

Arnuf looked unusually serious and shook his head.

'The Monk-father said they would be a friend to us in a time of great need,' he replied.

'This is a time of great need,' I said. 'It's time for lunch. And pass me the mead flask while you are at it. These biscuits are shrivelling my mouth. They're drier than a snake's side-pocket.'

That night we slept in a pile of stones which Arnuf had collected. I'd sent him off to fetch leaves but that half-wit cannot resist an interesting stone.

The next morning we made another hearty breakfast from our monk rations, and took to the track once again.

Dawn broke but the sun never climbed in the sky. We were higher up now and there was nothing for it but to trudge onwards into the cloud-murk.

Long we walked, cloaked by the freezing fog. I looked from ground to sky and sky to ground and could not tell them apart.

'Beowuff!' called Arnuf from somewhere in the mist ahead. Although I knew he was only a few steps away he could have been in Valhalla for all I knew.

'Arnuf! Stand still!' I called. A shiver of fear ran down my spine. What if he should wander off the track and slip down a cliff? The very thought made me shudder. For I had insisted that Arnuf carry the heavier pack – and inside it was the monk-gold and most of the food.

Ever so slowly – by means of repeated calling and careful tracking, I found my way to where my bewildered bench-mate sat.

'Let me help you with that burden,' I said gently, taking the pack from his back.

But he did not reply. He just sat with his snout in the air, staring into the distance.

'Well Arnuf, you have led us into a pretty pickle now,' I moaned looking around me. For we had come some way from the track, and now we stood on a goat-track or a deer-run or some other kind of path that starts off well but ends suddenly in disappointment.

'Arnuf!' I howled. 'We are lost!'

Arnuf did not move a muscle. He just stuck out his tongue and sat there

'Arnuf!' I yelled, in a rage. 'We've been caught by the cloud-murk, and we have little food or water and the streams are frozen. Thirst can kill as surely as any Dragon's axe.'

'There's one thing to be happy about,' he said.

'What's that?' I growled.

'The snow,' he said grinning. 'It really is snowing. I've been checking by sitting here and flake-catching.'

'What in the name of Thor's flashing bolts is flake-catching?' I asked.

'A game,' he laughed. 'I sit here and see if I can catch snowflakes in my mouth. Want to play?'

'Flake-catching?' I cried. 'You snow-blind slack-wit. The Ice-Queen has led us to our doom and you sit there catching her death-flakes on your tongue!'

'I think it's sticking,' he replied. 'I hope it sticks.'

I seized the pack and searched inside it for the mead flask. All that shouting had left me parched. But Arnuf had not tied it up properly, and all the mead had drained out, and turned our monk-biscuits to mush.

'Empty!' I moaned, turning the flask upside down and tipping out the last dribbles onto the ground.

'Want to make a snow eagle?' asked Arnuf.

Soon the snow was falling fast. Great thumping lumps of it, burning out the black of the mountain-rock and washing everything in white.

There was no way we could turn back and I could think of no other plan, so I started to dig a shelter. For a canny old Icelander called Snowlaf, that I once met on a slave-deck, told me that if you ever get caught out on the side of a mountain, the best thing you could do was dig yourself a snow-cave for a shelter. Snowlaf swore that once inside you'd be 'as warm as toast'.

'Linger outside on the mountainside,' he'd warned, 'and all your blood will rush to your head, freeze up and crack your brain-case.'

So I set my paws to the task of digging a snow-cave and before long, I'd carved out a large, uncomfortable ice-hollow. It had a doorway which I could block up with my pack to stop the snow blowing inside. However, when I shut the door, it was as dark as Hel's hearth-rug. Satisfied with my work, but in a bad temper, I slumped down and prepared for a long cold night.

I was soon woken up by a horrid howling from outside. At first I thought it was the vicious wind, so I shut my ears to it and clamped my hood tighter around my ears. I had a horror of wolves – for packs of the beasts are said to roam the hills, preying upon travellers and devouring them. They go for the tails first, according to the stories.

Soon, the howls turned into an annoying whine.

'Beowuff!' called my bench-mate. 'Is our snow-cave ready yet?'

'Be off with you! Go and play snow ravens on your own like I told you,' I replied.

'I'm tired of that game,' he moaned. 'Let me share your shelter.'

'Dig your own snow-home!' I cried. 'There's only room for one in here.'

'All right,' came the sad reply.

Now it was nearly dark outside and the wind was getting up. I sucked slowly on a mushy monk-biscuit.

'Beowuff?' came the shout.

'What now?' I answered.

'Can you help me to dig my own snow-hole?'

'Sorry!' I cried, peeping out of the shelter to get a better look at him.

The half-witted hound was covered in frost from his paws to his ice-caked ears. He looked like a frost-giant that had melted and shrunk.

'Listen carefully Arnuf, for this is important,' I said.

'Yes!'

'Be sure to dig your snow hole a little way down the mountainside, not too near mine.'

I had to give this order, for I didn't want to be swept away in a snow-fall.

'I will d-d-d-d-do as you s-s-s-say Beowuff,' he replied through chattering teeth.

'And Arnuf,' I said, 'If you see any yellow snow...'

'Yes?' he shivered.

'Be sure to eat it. It's the tastiest thing you'll find on this mountain tonight.'

'Yellow snow?' he said. 'I'll look out for it. Thanks.'

Arnuf began to dig frantically.

It was some time before I heard his voice again, blown up the slope on the searing wind.

'Beowuff! Beowuff!' he called.

'What?' I bellowed, only bothering to open my door half way this time. 'Don't tell me, you've found some yellow snow?'

'Yes. And I licked it all up,' he answered.

When it came to clumping great clod-wits, Arnuf really was the pick of the litter.

I pushed my pack back over the door of my snow-hole to cut out the icy wind.

I am not saying that all Icelanders are liars, but my frost blasted hollow was not nearly as 'snug,' as old Snowlaf the Icelander had promised it would be. It was colder than an ice-bear's bath in there.

Slowly, one by one, my paws went numb and I lost all feeling in my tail.

'Beowuff!' yapped Arnuf in excitement. 'I've found something. Come and see.'

Now, if any other dog than Arnuf had suggested that I step out of my shelter into the pitch dark to come and look at a sudden discovery he had made, I would have laughed and given him a 'No!' for my answer. If I poked my snout out, I'd soon find it staved in with a pole – and I'd freeze to death whilst my mate stole my snow-house. That is how bench-mates behave, where I grew up.

However, unlike me and my pack, Arnuf didn't have a lying bone in his body. So I dragged myself out of the hole, muttering oaths about leak-legged snow-oafs. When I got outside, I soon wished I hadn't. My front paws gave way and I toppled over into a snow drift. A drilling wind bored into my fur. It felt like I was coatless. I bounded through the drifts to where Arnuf's barks were coming from.

There, under the moonlight, I saw him standing at the bottom of a hole. Peering down into the frosty gloom, I saw that he was holding something in his jaws.

'Lend a paw and I'll share it with you!' he called, scrabbling about frantically.

'Arnuf! What in Thor's name are you're doing?'

'Digging out this sausage,' says Arnuf. 'We'll eat well tonight. It's a bit frozen, but it'll go nicely with that yellow snow.'

'Hold in the name of Heimdall!' I declared. 'That's no sausage.'

'Oh!' he cried in disappointment. 'What is it then?'

'That Arnuf... ' I explained, 'is a rope.'

'Oh!' he said dropping it back into the hole and looking at it with a puzzled face. 'Still, a rope might make for good gnawing eh? Something to get our teeth into.'

He wasn't fit to shovel snow from one place to another, as a coarse Norse poet once put it.

'Good gnawing?' I cried. 'Have all your brains rushed down to your gut-sack? Never mind gnawing, dig it out!'

The two of us set to digging. After I had made a start that showed some willing, I stopped and left Arnuf to do the work. For if hard labour was noble, Kings would dig their own fields.

I will say one thing for that useless sausage-sniffer Arnuf. He is a most marvellous digger. What he lacked in skill, he made up for with effort. His paws rose and fell like a Berserker's axe, sending plumes of snow shooting out from the hole.

Before long, he had discovered one end of the rope. It was nailed to a wooden stake, which had been driven deep into the ice.

'Oh!' said Arnuf. 'What do we do now we've found the end?'

'Every rope has two ends Arnuf,' I explained.

'So what do we do now?' he asked.

'We find the other end, you freeze-witted fool,' I answered.

Arnuf set to digging again and soon we were following the rope upwards and then along.

As I watched him working, I wondered what might be at the end of it. Knowing my luck, it was probably a poor traveller who had fallen off the mountain. We'd find his frozen body trussed up like a feast-day fowl.

But nothing could have prepared me for what I was about to discover.

All the time that Arnuf and I had been searching for the end of the rope, the blizzard had been skewering us against the mountainside. But all of a sudden, the wind died and the moon peeped out from behind the clouds, bathing the snow in a soft blue light.

I let out a cold gasp. I'd come some distance down the mountain. Now it would be impossible to make it back to the safety of my snow-cave.

Blurry shapes towered above me, but ahead I saw the thin line of a bridge leaping over a black chasm. It was shaggy with the thick frost.

'A bridge,' I cried. 'Look! We are saved!'

I jumped up, licking the bewildered Arnuf on the face. Then I remembered about his taste for yellow snow and I stopped licking him.

'A bridge?' said Arnuf. 'Why would a rope end in a bridge?'

'Because it's a rope bridge, you weak-witted whippet.'

CHAPTER EIGHT

ARCHER

Now, some of you might be wondering why the discovery this ice-clad crossing had me leaping around like a pup on his first pillaging trip. Well, high up on the other side of the chasm, I'd spotted a light.

I forgot my usual fear of high places and trotted across the bridge, happy as a chief's wife on a loot-day. My ice-gripped heart melted at the sight of that light, and began to pound as we drew nearer. The light was spilling through the battered door of a farmhouse.

I say 'farmhouse' but this was more of a crumbling hut, clinging to the hill with its last death-grip. If it wasn't frozen to the slope, I expect that the tumble-down cottage would have given up the struggle and flung itself down the mountain to end its agony.

My suspiciousness was beaten by the joy at the prospect of warmth, food and shelter. Even in the stifling cold, there was a funny scent about the place: both musky and mouldy at the same time.

Like a wise battle-Lord, I ordered my expendable friend to go ahead of me and knock on the door.

'Why should I do the knocking?' whined Arnuf.

'Because your face is friendlier than mine,' I snapped, shaking with the cold. 'Now get knocking before we freeze to death where we stand.'

Arnuf crept up to the hut but ran back whimpering.

'Did you knock?' I asked in excitement.

He shook his head.

'Beowuff...' he began, but before he could get his excuses ready, I gave him a good tongue-lashing.

'You cowardly Carl,' I cried, 'You dirt-digging danger-dodger! Anyone would think I was asking you to fight a troll, not knock on a farmhouse door!'

But my taunts fell upon deaf ears. Even when I threatened tell his new friends (the monks) about his behaviour, he refused to take another step.

I tried a bit more jeering and sneering but he just stood shivering and mumbling like a prayer-sayer. I even caught him fumbling with the cross-sticks that Fastwagger had given him.

'Alright!' I cried. 'You cower there in comfort, and I will dare the danger,' I called, strolling boldly towards the entrance. For my fear of the cold was greater than anything that was inside that hut.

As I got closer, the musty smell grew stronger and stronger. The place smelt worse than a newly dug death mound on a hot summer night. Holding my cloak over my nose, I stood shaking before the threshold, and was about to knock, but I pulled away my paw at the last moment. Something white was nailed to the door. I stood staring into a pair of hollow eye-holes as a flesh-picked skull leered back at me. I ran screaming back to Arnuf and dived bravely into a snow-pile.

'I tried to warn you Beowuff,' cried Arnuf in a dither. 'There's a death's head on that door. It is surely the house of an Outdweller.'

'A what-dweller?' I muttered, trying to calm my shattered nerves.

'One of the heathen fiends that Fastwagger and the Monk-father warned us about,' whined Arnuf.

'We're heathens ourselves!' I cried, recovering slightly. 'Don't be kitten-witted Arnuf. Sometimes I wish you were war-trained – I really do.'

Arnuf sniffed the air and let out another whimper.

'What if it's the house of an ice-giant?' he howled.

'Do you not think that the house of a giant would have a higher roof? You snow-bound slack-wit.'

'What if it belongs to one of the shorter Outdwellers,' he said. 'Some of them are tiny, you know.'

I sighed and shivered at the same time.

'Short Outdwellers?' I muttered. 'What are you babbling about?'

'It could be a soil-dwarf's set,' continued Arnuf.

'What in the name of the Bearded Bonefather is a 'soil-dwarf'?' I demanded.

It is said that even idiots speak the truth once a year. Judging by the smell, that hut could belong to any manner of short-legged dirt-digger.

'Soil dwarves are well known in Gutland. Have you not heard of them?' said Arnuf seriously. 'If they catch you poking your paw where it is not wanted, they'll pop up like a mole, sting you a good one and bite your limbs off.'

'Who told you that?' I sighed.

'My mother,' he replied. 'She was always warning me

about soil dwarves. And sand dragons.'

'It is a risk I am prepared to run,' I said, recovering my good sense. 'Would you rather live with no paws or freeze with all four intact?'

I did not wait for an answer, but instead, I balled up my courage, rushed back to the door and knocked hard. My three blows shook it on its oak hinges.

There was no answer.

I knocked again. This time, I said in a clear voice.

'I am a poor traveller lost in the snow – will you let me in to share your fire?'

'Nay!' answered a thin voice.

'Please!' I begged. 'I won't last the night.'

This much was true. The voice did not reply. Just as I was about to grovel some more it spoke again.

'Leave my hame. I give ye fair warning.'

Although the words were wary, the voice was as hard as iron and entirely without fear.

'I am not a robber,' I moaned. 'Just a traveller.'

'Save yer yap for one who'll believe ye,' it laughed.

'I will pay for your firewood,' I grovelled. 'Wait! I am putting a pile of gold coins by the door to show that I am in good faith.'

I pulled a paw full of gold from my loot-sack. But although my mind willed me to keep my promise and place it by the door, my jealous paws would not let go of my monk-geld. So I threw some stones down instead.

Arnuf shook his head.

'Ha!' laughed a voice like a bag of nails. 'Do ye take

me for a new-born ninny? "I am putting the geld by the door" he says!'

The voice fell silent and the wind sneered at me.

I was all out of sweetness and hearty talk, so I decided to try threats.

'All right! You have refused my offer and set me on an ill-course! I have no choice now but to take up this torch and burn you out of your 'hame'...' I snarled.

It was a desperate plan.

'Ah! I kenned it!' laughed the insider. 'Off gangs the weary traveller and now here's the threatener – come to rook me and wreck my hame.'

I waited before firing my final word-arrow.

'If I admit who I really am, can I come in and share your fire? I am already colder than the grave.' I begged. 'A winding-sheet would warm my bones.' Then I added 'If you refuse and I die here, my ghost will haunt your 'hame' forever.'

There are some in this world who think that their drinking horn is always half full and can see the good in everyone. And there are others who for whom the cup is always half-charged and think all the world is out to get them. The voice from behind the door belonged to the second sort of fellow.

Without waiting, I went on to plead my case.

'All right – I'll not talk falsely. Tonight I did come to rob you. Now in Bodin's name will you open the door? I am putting my knife down.'

'Ha!' said the insider. 'Do ye bide alane?'

'Sorry?' I mumbled, not understanding the question. He spoke much the same tongue as mine, but long years living in the mountains had blurred his words. I could only understand about half of what he said.

'Are ye alane? Or is there a whole longboat full of rooks out there?' he repeated.

This time I was careful with my answer.

'I did not come alone. I have a bench-mate with me. He is war-shy and of little use for anything but sneaking. I brought him along to help me carry away all of your worldly goods out of your 'hame' as you call it.'

There was a satisfied laugh, as if he had known that all along this was the case.

At long last, the wooden door opened and a voice called: 'Come on in then.'

I tumbled into the warmth and thrust my trembling face closer to his blazing fire. But before I could feel the relief of the warmth, something shot past me and stuck into to the wooden floor. I felt the rush of it as it whizzed past my nose and tore through my cloak. This happened again and again. When I tried to stand, five arrows pinned me to the floor by the cloak.

Before me stood a great horned beast. It smelt like a goat, but it was bigger than any goat I have ever seen. Granted, most of the goats I've seen have been oozing fat over a long-fire or cut to pieces in a cook-pot.

This one was too big for any spit or skewer in a king's hall. He was grey bearded and in his cloven hooves he held an enormous longbow. It was pointing straight at my eyes. I flinched and edged backwards.

His hovel, for you could not call it a house, was lined with wolf skins. The air was thick with the musty scent of goats. As I clamped my nose shut against the smell, I saw that the archer had long iron knives strapped to each end of his bow.

'Call yer freend,' he ordered.

But in my panic I didn't realise what he meant.

'Say that again? I begged. 'I'm hard of hearing.'

'Yer freend,' he repeated. 'He's ootside. D'ya ken?'

Sadly, I did not 'ken'. It was hopeless. I had no clue what he was talking about.

The bow glided smoothly as the archer adjusted his aim, and his gimlet eyes never left mine.

'Get callin!'

'Don't shoot!' I whimpered. 'Help! Arnuf! Arnuf!'

As my weak-witted friend entered, another arrow leapt from his dreadful bow and tore through my cloak, pinning me back down with force.

Being a weak-wit has its advantages, for Arnuf seemed delighted with the archer's dart work.

'Nice arrows!' said Arnuf. 'Where did you learn to shoot like that?'

'You'll see,' muttered the archer, grimly.

A serious expression passed over Arnuf's face

'We could use your help on our Quest. We seek Heroes. Never before have I seen bow work like that.'

The archer did not answer but slid his arm into a bag and began to coil something about his arm.

For once, my weak-witted friend had blundered onto the right path. The bow is one of my favourite weapons. The sagas call it 'the coward's choice' for the same reason that I like it. For an archer can rain down merry death upon his enemy, whilst keeping well out of range of his broadsword or blood-axe. Could we persuade him to take up the monks' cause?

'My friend speaks true,' I said warmly. 'We've come on a Quest from the Sine Carne Order – a peace loving monk-pack. Their pockets are bursting with geld and relics. They'll reward any hero that joins…'

'Shut yer yap,' he ordered.

A rope streaked through the air and I felt something fall around my neck. I clawed at my throat but the more I struggled, the tighter it held me.

'Nae more chatter, or it'll tak yer breath,' he said.

It was not very long before the archer had both Arnuf and I securely tethered to posts on each wall of the hall. When our ropes were tied to his satisfaction, he trotted out into the freezing night, without another word.

'It's warm in here,' called Arnuf across the hut.

He was right. For the first time in days, I could feel my paws. My ears had started to thaw out, leaving me with an aching brain-case. I was trying to think, but it was impossible with Arnuf yapping on like a fish seller.

'What's that archer up to?' called Arnuf. 'Will he join our Quest to help the meatless monks?'

'Meatless monks!' I growled. 'If there was an order of Brainless Brothers, they'd make you the blessed

Monk-father.'

My backward bench-mate thought about this for a few moments. 'Abbot Arnuf the Empty-Headed' that's what they'd call you! Of course he's not going to join our Quest. You... cross-stick clutching clot-head!'

I would have raged on for longer, but the twine around my neck was growing tighter, making me cough like a beached-whale.

'What's he up to then?' asked Arnuf.

'How in the name of Thor's bolts should I know? He's probably gone to fetch his throat-slitting kit.'

Arnuf let out a horrified whimper.

Then the door opened, letting in a freezing blast.

But it was not the archer with his favourite gutting knife. Instead, a herd of mountain goats of various shapes and sizes trotted in and packed the hovel to bursting. The ripe tang of wild goat stuck in my throat. One of them trod on my foot and I let out a curse.

'Beg yer pardon,' it bleated.

'Hello!' said Arnuf. 'Who are you?'

'I'm called Billi,' answered the creature, turning to address my bench-mate. 'Are you helping Father?'

Arnuf touched his cross-sticks and nodded.

The little goat seemed pleased.

'Thank ye,' he said. 'The pack grow stronger every day. Today they nearly caught me by the stream...'

'Quiet!' boomed a familiar voice. 'Nae more talk with these strangers. They mean ye nae good.'

As the kid bleated his apologies, I felt a bump on the brain-case and everything went dark.

CHAPTER NINE

HOWL

As the archer tore the sack off my head, a dazzling whiteness bit into my eyes and the wind whistled straight up my snout. He thrust something towards my mouth.

'Dreenk,' he ordered.

I hesitated. It didn't smell too good. 'Gang on and dreenk,' he said again. 'It's all ye'll get.'

'Er, thank you but no!' I answered.

'Suit yersen,' muttered the archer. Then he stomped off into the blinding snow.

It was a tight pass. Our bearded hut-mate had roped us to a stake. Its ice-clad wood provided the only splash of colour in this frozen white Nifelheim.

I shaded my eyes and squinted as the archer strode off down the track. A stinging silence spread across the land. The ice held the mountains in a cold embrace. Every now and again you could hear it cracking. To my ears, it sounded like mad laughter.

I tracked the archer's shape for a few moments but before long he was lost in the snow-glare.

'Beowuff,' whined a voice at my side.

'What?' I growled.

'Where's our friend gone?'

'How in the name of Freya the Slayer should I know?' I replied.

'Beowuff,' came the voice again. 'I'm cold.'

The wind blew. My spine shuddered. My thoughts turned to Outdwellers. Who knows what creatures Arnuf's mindless moaning might attract?

'Shut your meatless mead-hole!' I cried. 'I'm frozen too, but there's no use howling about it.'

A wind-gust blew another of his wails to my ears.

'Stop whining Arnuf,' I ordered. 'I am not in jest.'

'I'm not whining,' replied Arnuf. 'It's you. You're the one who is doing the howling.'

'I am not!' I answered in an injured tone. 'Shut your snout, or you'll wake the ice-giants. You won't be laughing when they use your frozen legs for fang picks.'

The wind dipped and another lonely howl rang across the valley. It was answered by a dreadful chorus.

'How did you do that?' asked Arnuf.

'I didn't!' I wailed, clawing at the rope in a panic.

'What was it then?' he shuddered.

'Wolves!' I moaned, struggling at the ropes again. 'There's a whole pack of them, by the sound of it.'

'Wolves? Here? In the mountains?' exclaimed Arnuf in astonishment.

'Where in Frey's name do you think wolves live?' I thundered. 'In the town? In little golden cages?'

'Wolf! Help!' cried Arnuf, cringing like a cat-licker.

'Shut your yap,' I moaned.'

'Wolf! Wolf! Help,' he cried again.

The wolves howled back in a mocking answer.

'Don't let them eat me!' howled Arnuf.

I wondered if Arnuf's fat head would be enough to satisfy this hell-pack.

'Dig Arnuf! Dig!' I cried, scrambling at the frozen ground. 'We stand no chance if we are trussed up here like a pair of fattened geese.'

Arnuf clawed at the ice till his paws were ragged but it was harder than stone.

I searched the hillside. There was no sign of the pack of prey-takers, but their howls grew ever louder. Would they wait for sundown, before coming in for their dinner?

'The stake is frozen solid. I can't dig it out,' moaned Arnuf. 'What do we do now Beowuff?'

'Get your cross-sticks out and start praying,' I sighed.

Arnuf let out a frightened yelp.

A pair of yellow eyes peered out of the shadows. Soon they were joined by another pair and then another until the hillside was dotted with glowering peep-holes.

Then the howling started again. It was worse than a herd of cats in a giant's caldron.

The first pair of eyes moved towards me. There was a cold will behind their fiery gaze, as if they knew I was defenceless.

'Wolf! Wolf! Help!' barked Arnuf.

'Shut your yap,' I ordered. 'Don't you know the tale of the little pup who cried "wolf"?'

'No,' replied Arnuf. 'What happened to him?'

'Keep on howling like that and you'll find out,' I growled.

At that point, I stopped telling him to be silent. I decided that the beasts might take Arnuf first if he yelped louder than me. But I've never known a starving wolf to refuse a second helping. Our best chance was to stand together or better still, I might persuade my bench-mate to stand between those red-fanged killers and my trembling throat.

Inevitably, there came a horrible growling and the first wolf approached. It is said that in wild packs the leader eats first, but this was a she-wolf with a little pup at her side.

Arnuf brightened at the sight of the mother and child.

'Look! She's got her little one with her,' he cooed. The tiny wolf cub trotted up to our stake, and began to eye Arnuf fiercely.

'What's your mother doing, little fellow?' asked Arnuf.

'Teaching him how to kill, most likely,' I replied.

Before these words were out of my maw, the wolf had started to lunge at Arnuf. It was so small that its attack was no more than a play-fight. All the while, it let out a weak growl. After a few practice lunges, it grew tired of the game and curled up its snout to reveal a set of pearly white teeth.

'Look he's smiling!' said Arnuf. 'I think he likes me!'

Before I could prevent it, he stretched out a paw to pat the wolfling on the head.

The tiny brute snarled and snapped at his paw.

'There's a good little wolf!' said Arnuf.

But I wasn't the only one watching the weak-witted wolf-charmer in wonder and disbelief.

'Careful,' I cried. 'Its mother is looking at you.'

With a growl that would have woken Hel from her death-bed, the she-wolf crouched back, swung open her jaws and sprang at Arnuf's throat.

I cannot bear the sight of blood, so I closed my eyes. I heard a twang and a thwack and a thud. When I opened my eyes again, the she-monster lay snout down in the snow, with an arrow through its throat.

Then I heard a savage growl. An enormous he-wolf had come. He froze my heart with a look of loathing. In an instant, I knew who he blamed for her death.

'It wasn't me! No!!' I wailed, cringing like a captured Swede. But it was hopeless. The pack-father bent himself back like a bowstring and came at me. His claws racked that air, streams of hot drool flying from his gaping maw. His jaws were throat high as his cruel fangs searched for their target, hungry as a head-taker's axe.

Without another sound, he crashed stricken onto the ice. As I backed away from the twitching mountain of grey fur, I spied a long arrow sticking through his side.

'Stand still!' came a cry from half way up the hill.

Our bow-twitching captor was on a wolf hunt, and he was using us as the bait in his trap.

One wolf-Lord after another leapt forth to avenge their fallen king and queen. One by one they fell in their tracks until the hill was strewn with the grey-furred monsters. It was a good thing that he'd tied me to the stake, because I'd have flung myself off an ice-cliff to avoid the terrible fangs of those beasts.

When it was over, the Archer came down to inspect his kills. I expected him to stagger down the hill, pleased as a loot-day pillager. But he seemed to take no pleasure in his victory as he set to work with his skinning knife.

'Farewell Wolf-Laird,' he said slowly, pausing over the body of the fallen leader. 'Tis' pity ye and yer kin should have to die. But yer pack grew too strong...'

Soon he had Arnuf and I tied to a sledge and we dragged the freezing body of the wolf-Lord back to the Archer's shack so that he could 'tak trophies.'

That night, as we feasted on his thin gruel, I battered my brain-case dreaming up ways to escape. The archer warned us to expect a 'morn of toil' tomorrow. I do not know what he had planned, but I could not bear another wolf-hunt. At last, Fate threw me a bone. For the Archer went outside the hut to do some skinning, leaving Arnuf and I alone with the goats. The smallest of the goats was also the most inquisitive. I was just thinking of a way to get him talking, when Arnuf spoke.

'What is there to do around here?' he asked.

'Do?' bleated the kid, eyeing him suspiciously.

'For fun,' barked Arnuf. 'In my village, we make toy ships, or hold digging contests. Or go crow stoning.'

'We never do anything like that,' said the kid. 'Father does nae hold with it.'

A cold wind drilled in through a hole in the door.

'Why not?' I asked.

'Play is a waste of the warm,' father says. 'He likes

to set me tasks and there's nae time for anything else.'

'What about in the summer? Surely you must play games in the summer?'

'This is the summer!' said the little goat. 'You should try it here in winter. We bide inside fer weeks on end.'

'Your poor thing,' said Arnuf. 'You should see Gutland in the summer months.'

When I heard Arnuf say this, I had to bite my tongue and dig myself in the belly to stop myself laughing. You can tell it's summer in Gutland when the stones on the beach dry up. Perhaps the wind may dip for a week, in which case the stink of the fetid fens turns the air sour. No wonder Gutlanders go off raiding every summer.

But the little goat was all ears for tales of the Farlands, as he called them.

'Tell me about your hame,' he begged.

'It's nice,' said Arnuf.

I knew I could not leave the task of tempting the kid with tales to my slack-tongued bench-mate.

'Gutland? There are no words to tell of its wonders. You need to see it with your own two eyes to believe it!' I declared. 'This old verse says it best...'

Hear you, hill dweller,
of Gutland's far off shores,
Castles of grass,
Sun-spears green as emeralds,
Happy friends to greet the weary traveller,
Wolf-free hills where the wildflowers dance,
Grass sweeter than King's mead,

Sun as warm as your hearth-fire,
Corn-fat fields laden with gleaming gold,
In merry Lord Ruffgar's Gutland home.

I let the last line trail off in the manner of a hall-singer.

Arnuf let out a melancholy howl of approval.

'Beowuff, that was, very... nice!' he sniffed.

'Dinnae stop!' cried the goat. 'Gang on! Castles of grass! For all the world, I could do with a taste o' that stuff!'

Now I know how the Skalds feel. I had completely run out of good things to say about Gutland.

Before I could make any excuses, the icy wind tore the door open, almost busting it off its hinges. In the doorway stood a horned head, clutching in its cloven hoof the wolf-trophies that he had been busy skinning.

He trotted right up to me, arrowing a furious glance at the kid. Throwing a wolf-head into the corner, he crouched down and spat on the blade of his skinning knife, measuring it against my neck.

'Silence!' he ordered. 'Another word and I'll skin the pair of ye.'

The thought of this set my heart flapping like a winged pigeon. I let out a whimper and slunk back into the corner of the hut.

Then the Archer turned towards his son and went on in a kinder tone. 'Did I nae tell ye not tae speak with these strangers? They mean ye nae good lad.'

Chapter ten

Three Goat Broth

The next day was the same as the last save for three things: the archer grew meaner: his stew grew thinner; and the pile of wolf-heads rose like a bloody wallflower in the far corner of our ice-clad 'hame'.

I wondered how much more of this I could stand. I did not dare speak openly with the kid again, but twice I caught his gaze and begged him to set me free.

That night, I dropped exhausted to my cold corner and sank immediately into a welcome dream. Then I heard a voice in my ear.

'Beowuff! Beowuff!' it seemed to whisper.

'Not now Ethelpelt,' I moaned.

'Wake up! We're escaping!' yapped Arnuf.

I rose to find the fire dead and the cold gnawing chunks out of the hut and everything inside it.

With white cloud-breath billowing from my mouth, I peered over the piles of wolf-skins to the far corner where the Archer usually slept. It was empty.

'Don't worry. He's gone off hunting,' said Arnuf.

My paw ran to the place on my throat, where he'd stroked me with his skinning knife.

'Are you sure?' I whined.

'Father's taken his bow,' bleated an excited voice.

The kid had gnawed through the leather twine that tethered Arnuf to his wall, and was already busy doing a similar job on my leash.

'Castles of grass!' cried the goat. 'I cannae wait to eat them.'

'Er Beowuff, I can explain...' began Arnuf.

'No need,' I laughed.

My weasel-words had taken their time to work. But the kid had come around to thinking that he would rather risk death with a pair of strangers than spend another night in an ice-house with his grim father.

If our young friend had gnawed me free first, I would have grabbed some stores and a waterskin and bolted for it, without a moment's thought for the other two. But as he gnawed at the leather cord that held me, my scheming brain got to work in earnest.

'Corn-fat fields,' whispered our new trail-mate in excitement. 'Are we ganging off straight to Gutland?'

'Aye,' I lied, as my belly gave out a growl. 'But we'll need to take some food, for it is a long road.'

'Wait!' blurted my bench-mate. 'Don't you think that the young one should tell his father where he's going?'

When Arnuf's wits went into to battle, common sense fled the field.

'Tell his father?' I growled. 'What do you think the Archer will do if he finds us? Wave farewell to us with his skinning knife? Keep your stupid snout shut, unless you want an arrow in it.'

Fortunately the kid knew better.

'Father must never know,' he said in earnest. 'He has a evil temper. Ye've nae seen the like of it.'

'Get packing. Make haste!' I ordered. 'We'll need food and water for two weeks.'

The kid darted around the shack, crashing about like an ice-giant. At last he found a couple of waterskins. But he left the cauldron and the other valuables, bleating that his father would need them.

While he was busy with this, I scoured the hut for the bag with the monk's geld in it. I was about to abandon my search when at last I found it, stashed under a stack of wolf-skins.

Meanwhile, the kid had got hold of another food-sack and filled it with dried roots and honey-biscuits and various tasty treats for the journey.

The kid had also packed a leather pouch full of the mixture which his father used to make our daily soup. I'd assumed that we were being fed on left-over scraps, but our guardian was actually eating it too. No wonder he'd lost his belly-lust. A few days in that horrid-hut had almost frozen my taste buds. As I sniffed the mixture, I wondered if it would improve the taste of goat-flesh.

'Follow me friends!' I cried. 'For we must leave this place, and take the road for Gutland with great haste.'

'Beowuff...' began my thin-witted bench-mate.

'What?' I snapped, snatching up the waterskins and tieing them on to my pack.

'I long to see dear old Gutland again, but have you forgotten the vow that we have made?'

'No,' I lied. 'What vow was that?'

'Our promise to help the monks of Sin Carne,' said

Arnuf solemnly, clutching at his cross-sticks.

Those meatless mead-sippers had been frozen out of my thoughts for days.

'Have no fear. For we will save the monks of Sin Carne as well.'

'How can we do that if we are Gutland bound?' asked Arnuf.

'You swore ye'd tak me to Gutland!' moaned the kid.

'By Bodin's beard, shut your bleat-holes. The pair of you are yammering like a couple of she-cats! Have patience,' I snarled. 'I have it – we'll pop back to the meatless monastery... on the way to Gutland! There, are you both happy? Now let us be off before the Archer returns and uses us for pin sticking practice.'

'Tell me stories of yer Gutland hame, while we walk,' begged the goat.

More Gutland tales? I would sooner have strangled the kid there and then rather than make up more drivel about Arnuf's stoney homeland. But I fretted that the kid's knife-weilding father would return to his own 'hame' and discover us kidnapping his son, and take two more trophies to place atop his stack of wolf-heads.

So I ushered my companions out of that ice-cracked hovel, and began to spout a sea of drivel.

I cannot remember it all, but I think that it included the following: giant forests of sugar-grass; honey pools for wading, splashing and drinking. Exquisitely decorated goat-maidens capering through the flower-strewn slopes in the warmth of the gentle Gutland sun.

Arnuf had lived all of his days in Gutland. Wasn't it odd that he'd never seen its cherry-lakes or carefully shaved goat-maidens? Yet throughout this storm of nonsense, he smiled pleasantly, his thick head nodding in agreement, bobbing like a moored longboat.

I broke off in order to talk directions with the kid. He had heard about a pass through the mountains which was to be found somewhere to the South. So we followed this road southwards for an hour before I thought it best to turn eastwards and make our trail harder to follow. I had not forgotten the Archer. He might already be on our tails.

The ice-track narrowed as we wound our way up into the nameless peaks, until it was 'as thin as an axe's lips' as the Skalds would put it. On we walked, until our paws were frozen. I feared that the path would run out inexplicably in the middle of nowhere, as such sprite-tracks often do.

I was never at peace, for there was the ever-present fear that the arrow-slinger might be stalking up behind us. Or worse still, that the silence would be cracked by the call of a ravenous wolf pack.

Despite this constant terror, there is something about a stoney land – all those barren slopes and cold hills – which sets the stomach grumbling.

As the weak sun dipped behind a range of name-less peaks we settled down for the night. I snatched the food sack from Arnuf and tipped out its contents onto the barren ground. My mouth filling with slaver at the thought of the treats. But when I looked at the food pile, it soon dried up. Was this all we had? A pile of gnarled roots, purple in colour. And a stack of shield-hard biscuits, frozen harder than the rocks on a Gutland beach.

None of this would calm my raging hunger. Then I had a wicked thought. What my gut-sack craved was meat! I had not tasted it for weeks.

A warming bowl of goat broth would do me, followed by a roasted goat steak. I also had a nice recipe for three goat bake but I could make do with one goat at a pinch. So what if Arnuf disapproved? He could feast on ice-biscuits for all I cared. Besides – would it not be best to get rid of the evidence of our kidnapping? If the Archer caught us, we would feel the force of his wrath.

With murder in my eyes, and drool filling my mouth, I looked longingly at the sleeping kid. In my meat-mad mind, I'd made a meal of him already. My paw reached to my side, groping for my blade. Then I remembered – the archer had taken our weapons and locked them away in his store-chest. I had no throat-cutter to do the deed with. Cursing, I snatched up the empty food sack. Then I caught the kid by his legs, stuffed a gag in his bleat-hole, and flung him inside the sack.

With a churning belly, I wondered how to do the vicious dead. Then something unusual happened. A thin beam of sunlight appeared from behind a cloud. On the path above me, a little string of silver snaked down from the snowy heights. It was the prettiest sight I'd seen for days.

'A mountain stream!' I cried. 'I'll drown him!' Snatching up the sack with the struggling goat inside, I strode up the path to the sparkling water and thrust the bag down with force.

But alas! The stream was not of drowning depth. It was little more than a trickle against the black rocks.

Frustrated, I sat down upon a boulder. The world around me was still and all was at peace, save for the bleating of the angry goat inside the bag.

Across the stream I saw an unusual sight. It was an ancient gorse bush, its age-thickened branches twisted like rope. A beam of sunlight shone out, tearing through the mist like a weird-light. For a moment, I could have sworn that the bush was on fire.

'A burning bush!' I cried. 'I'll roast him!'

Snatching up the bag with the kid inside, kicking like a hill-horse, I picked my way through the thorns.

After some thought, I realised that the old gorse bush was not really on fire, it was only a trick of the eye, so I returned to the track with some brushwood for a fire.

It is not easy to burn a goat on narrow mountain path. Even as I started the fire, I knew that my plan was doomed. It would barely singe Billi's goat-beard.

I slumped down, exhausted. With a heavy heart, I picked up a frozen biscuit from the food pile. It looked more toothsome than the roots.

I held the biscuit close to my tiny fire and waited. For all of my flesh-lust, it looked as if there would be no meat on the menu tonight.

Then, I saw it. A great pile of stones and rocks on the

hillside above us. The snows around them had melted. A branchless pine stood like a flag-staff. One slender branch held the rocky host in place.

'Rocks' I cried. 'If I can get these stones rolling, I can crush the little bleater!'

For goat meat is tough – a rockfall would make it tender. I could tear off strips and cook them on sticks.

Leaving the goat wriggling in the bag, I crept past the sleeping Arnuf, climbed up to the pine tree and hauled with all my might. The branch came out of the rock-pile and a large chunk of the mountain gave way.

Flapping like a spooked hen, I jumped back. I feared I'd be swept off the cliff by the falling rocks.

As the dust settled I rubbed my belly and climbed down to inspect my wicked work.

Then the thin hillside air rang with my curses. The goat was still there in the bag, untouched! Half the mountain had rolled past it but it had come through the rock storm without even losing a hair on its chin.

'Is all well?' called Arnuf in a frightened voice.

His first thought was for the kid. He howled like a wounded wolf when he saw the pile of rocks.

I let out a howl. To my horror, the sack with all of our food had been swept away down the hillside.

'Billi!' moaned Arnuf. 'Billi! Where are you?'

Spotting the sack in the middle of the rock pile, Arnuf raced over and untied it.

When the kid crept out, he begged for water.

'What happened?' he bleated. 'I was asleep, dreaming of Gutland and...'

'There was a rockfall,' I explained. 'Thank Bodin you are safe.'

Later, as he slept by the fire, Arnuf took me aside.

'Why was Billi in that sack?' he asked accusingly.

'He was tired,' I explained. 'So I decided to carry him. To give his little legs a rest.'

'Are you telling the truth?' he demanded.

'Yes, I swear it,' I lied.

'Billi's mouth was bunged up with a cloth,' growled Arnuf accusingly.

'What of it?' I replied. 'I lent him the cloth. He wanted to save his voice for singing by the fireside.'

'I see. I am sorry I doubted you Beowuff,' he said.

'Arnuf!' I said. 'Do you see those gulls over there on the hill? You're more gullible than any of that feather-brained flock. I am too tired to lie so I'll admit it. I got into a bit of a meat-sweat and I wanted to cook Billi.'

'Beowuff!' snapped Arnuf in disgust, clutching at the monk-sticks at his collar 'Beowuff? How could you?'

'Wait,' I replied. 'That kid is possessed. He's just like one of Thor's goats from the sagas. The ones that can come back to life and cheat death. Three times I've tried to kill Billi, and three times he's survived. Each time it has gone ill for me. Just look at our empty cooking pot.'

'Swear!' demanded Arnuf, clutching at his cross-sticks.

'Swear what?' I asked.

'Swear on your life that you won't eat Billi.'

CHAPTER ELEVEN

HEL'S BELLS

The weak sun was high in the sky.

'Beowuff! Wake up!' cried my bench-mate.

In order to put temptation out of my path, Arnuf had decided that it would be best if he and Billi went off together to hunt for anything that would go in a goatless stew. Now they were busy tipping their forage into a pile by the cooking pot. I don't know how he did it, but the bearded bleater had gone down the mountainside and rescued our stew-pot from under the fallen rocks.

'What's for supper?' I asked greedily. 'I could eat a whole village.'

'Rich pickings,' said Arnuf.

'There's enough roots for a stew,' added the goat.

'Did you get any meat?' I asked, clutching my belly.

'Nay,' answered the goat, eying me suspiciously.

'Look what I've found,' called Arnuf.

My guts stated to rumble.

'Is that meat?' I enquired.

'Of a kind,' he replied.

'Of what kind?' I sighed, ready for disappointment.

'It's ground meat!' said Arnuf.

I stuck my nose into his food- sack and sniffed. It smelled gamey, but I didn't like the look of it.

'Ground-meat?' I muttered. 'That doesn't sound very toothsome.'

'Wait till you've tasted it,' said Arnuf.

He tipped out the sack and a pile of greyish strips spilled onto the path. 'My granny used to swear by ground-meat,' he added.

I was so hungry that I was willing to believe it was fit for eating. I picked up one of the strips in my maw but the next thing he said stopped me mid mouthful.

'Poor old granny...' he whined.

'Why? What happened to her?' I asked. 'She didn't die of poisoning did she?'

'No,' said Arnuf in an injured tone. 'She went mad.'

Just then, Billi came trotting up. When he saw Arnuf's ground-meat, he let out an alarmed bleat.

'Toadstools! Dinnae eat that!' he warned.

'Toadstools?' I said, eying Arnuf accusingly.

'Aye,' said the kid. 'That grey-cap there is named Hel's Bell, or Helscap. Lick it and you'll gang away to meet the Hiddenfolk and their wee pink rabbits.'

'Pink rabbits?' exclaimed Arnuf. 'They sound fun.'

'They are not real rabbits, you weak-wit!' I barked. 'He means if we eat that 'ground-meat' of yours, we'll start seeing things.'

'For truth?' said Arnuf excitedly. 'I've always fancied myself as a seer of visions. The Second Sight runs in our family, you know.'

'Don't tell me,' I sighed. 'Your mad granny had it?'

Arnuf stared at me in amazement, as if I was a witch who had suddenly dropped from the sky.

'How did you know that? Do you have the Second Sight too?' he asked in wonder.

'What happens after you see the pink rabbits?' I asked, grabbing hold of Arnuf's snout and snapping it tightly shut to stop him tasting the ground-meat.

'You'll get cramps in yer gut-sack,' said the kid. 'Then there's hot sweats, then the night-terrors come.'

'Did you hear that?' I said, rapping Arnuf on the snout-hole.

Whining, he dropped the toadstool and started to pack the rest of the pile of Helscaps back into the sack.

'What in the name of Thor's self-swinging sword do you think you are doing?' I demanded.

'Saving them for later,' whined the weak-wit.

'Saving them?' I growled. 'Saving your deadly poisonous toadstools... for later!!!'

Letting out a snarl, I seized the sack and shook the rest of the foul things out onto the ground.

'They're poisonous – but nae 'deadly' poisonous,' said Billi, in the tone of a village know-it-all.

'Where did you learn so much about it?' I asked.

'From father,' he said proudly. 'Did yer father nae learn ye aboot herbs and roots?'

'My father was not wise in herb-lore,' I said. Actually, he was not wise at all. The only knowledge he passed on got me banished for raiding my King's bone-hoard.

'So you're a trained herb-picker Billi? How useful,' said Arnuf.

I agreed. We could send the little bleater down the hill to collect some leaves and then boil him up in a broth made of his own forage.

'With Billi to lead us, we can live off the land,' said

Arnuf. 'He can point us towards the right plants and we will gather them up and eat them.'

Even flea-wits like Arnuf stumble on a good idea every once in a mad-moon.

'Tell us – my good goat-guide,' I began. 'What toothsome plants and roots are there for a dog to eat, here in the mountains of your home?'

'Very few,' said the goat, 'now the snow has come.'

The Skalds sing that the Goddess Hel has a empty plate called hunger. Now my belly burned with its cold fire. I pointed at a flock of birds in the distance.

'Sea birds,' I cried. 'Cormorants by the look of them. They'd go down a treat.'

Billi looked at me in disgust.

'Can ye stomach raw sea-bird?' he croaked.

'Right now, I am so hungry that I could stomach raw seagull's stomach,' I answered.

So we left the path and went on a bird hunt. The way was not easy. Not for us dogs at any rate, although our goat-guide sprang from rock to rock with ease and was not bothered by the thorns. No wonder goat meat tastes so tough, the bleating beggars must have skins of iron.

My pads were red-raw by the time I'd picked my way through to the bottom of a rock-strewn gorge. I looked around to find myself in the very middle of nowhere. If a wandering beggar were to pick up a pebble and hurl it off a cliff – this was the sort of place it would land. It was a treeless, pathless, charmless land-scrap, grim as a Gutland grave-mound.

'It's great to get off the path,' called Arnuf. 'Now we can get to see the real country.'

Every now and again we caught sight of the wheeling flock of gulls, tempting us with their cries. I feared they would fly off and leave us in the middle of the wild, so I willed my legs to carry me onwards along the gorge. The goat led the way and Arnuf dawdled along at the rear, grinning like a loon.

As I trudged, I cursed him soundly. I was busy thinking of a new name to call him when I spotted something under a moss covered boulder. It was pile of bone-sticks and rag-scraps. I stuck my starving tongue in and gave it a lick. But the bones were cracked and sand dried by countless summers. It would be easier to suck the marrow out of a stone.

Then my greedy eye spied something gleaming under the bone-pile. So I poked my thieving snout in to have a closer look. It was a key. The gold was Irish by the look of it.

A bleat of warning rang in my ears.

'Leave that be,' said Billi.

'Have you bashed your beardy brain-case on a boulder?' I cried. 'It's treasure – gold by the look of it.'

''Tis dead-geld! Leave it for the Hiddenfolk.'

'The Hiddenfolk?' I scoffed.

'You know,' said Arnuf, who had caught up with us. 'The Hiddenfolk. Wraiths of the mountains: Ice giants and the trolls and that lot.'

'I know who he means,' I replied.

'Tis dead-geld. It belongs to them now,' said Billi in a hushed voice.

'Ice giants and trolls! Tales to make pups stay close to the long-fire,' I laughed.

'Watch this,' I said, extending a shaking paw to touch my prize.

The mountains looked on stone-faced as I snatched their forbidden gold.

Then there came a bellow, like an angry dragon rising from his treasure-heap. It rang through the gorge, louder than a war-horn, blasting from wall to wall.

I have often thought that I am led through life by two ropes: the lead of greed and the leash of fear.

This time, the fear-leash won the day and I decided it would be best to leave the golden key for the Hiddenfolk, just in case there were any about. The kid's warning had awoken the cowardly cur in me.

I thanked the stars and moon as I walked away. What if I had stolen the key to a stone-troll's cave, or a wraith's gate?

Later, as we set up camp, the thought of that key played on my mind. What treasures might it unlock?

When the night was old, I left the others sleeping and picked my way back down the track. I'd almost given up my search when I spotted the boulder with the white moss, shining under the moon. My heart came up to my belly as I thought about the key's owner.

I searched the hills for any sign of the Hiddenfolk – but I stood in the ancient silence with only the rocks and brushwood for company.

Soon the key was in my loot-sack and I was trotting back down the track to the camp. If the others missed me I'd tell them that I'd gone in search of water.

Later, I woke to the sound of that dreadful bellowing again – only it was weaker this time. My paw crept to the key, safe now in my loot-sack, but the noise soon passed.

We breakfasted on a frozen rat which we'd found on the path. But it had been thin – it had probably starved to death. The goat found some snow berries but he ate them all before I could get my paws on them.

My thoughts ran to the treasure. For I had decided my key would unlock a great chest full of gold. Right now I would have given all of Bodin's geld-heap for a decent deer steak.

I was just thinking that a goat steak would also do when we rounded a bend in the gorge and came to a swiftly flowing river. Suddenly, we caught sight of the wheeling birds again, they were closer than before.

'Why are those ravens flocking over there on the beach?' asked Arnuf. 'Are they pecking at a slain-pile?

'Those are not ravens,' I said.

'How do you know?' demanded my companion.

'Have you ever seen a white raven?' I sighed. 'They're impossibly rare. But not half as rare as the sound of good-sense coming from your silly snout-hole.'

Arnuf gave me his puzzled look.

'Don't just stand there!' I cried. 'Catch them!'

Fearful that the birds would flap off to freedom – I raced towards that feathered flock. When the first of them took off, I spotted an old oak barrel. The gulls had been trying to beak-out some kind of tasty treat from inside. The thought of those winged sky-pigs feasting on this find sent me berserk. I rushed at the wooden prize, hurling rocks at the gulls.

As I got closer, my heart sank like a scuttled sea-cutter. The barrel was leaking fish. The high reek of cod hit my snout. It was not a perfect catch. If a cat had sniffed this fish at a market, it would have moved to the next stall. But in my starved state I was happy to turn fish-eater and guzzle them up like a Gutland tom.

'Flap off! That's mine!' I shouted, but the cursed birds paid no heed. Howling with fury, I took aim and threw my last stone at a nearby gull. Normally, I am a second rate slinger. But this gull-Lord was enormous, and my flint-stone cracked him right on the beak-hole. He let out a piercing squawk. Then the rest of the flock rose like one great animal and took to the sky, wheeling and swooping down upon me like crazed Valkiries.

'Help! Help! Arnuf!' I cried, shielding my face to avoid their rage.

'Come on! Gang this way,' bleated Billi. He'd discovered a crack in the wall of the gorge. Blowing like a beached whale, I dived inside, out of reach of that sharp beaked mob.

'Make way for me,' called Arnuf.

'Find your own cave!' I barked, not daring to budge.

'Aaargh!' came a cry. Peeping out from my hiding-hole, I saw that two black-headed gulls had cornered Arnuf by the river. Another one flapped down and began to beak him mercilessly on the snout.

'Arnuf! Tae me!' cried a noise from behind. With a shrieking charge, Billi sprang out and horn-butted the biggest one.

'Squeeze up Beowuff. Mak room fer us!' bleated the fighting goat.

Reluctantly, I budged up. The cave was a good deal bigger than I had first thought. There was a large dark opening to my left. Arnuf slumped down in the corner, whimpering in his usual war-shy way.

As the sun rose, the smell of the salted cod drifted over to our hide out. For some time I lay in silence watching the gulls stuff their gullets. But soon my belly could stand it no longer. Mad with gut-lust, I sprang up and made a desperate rush for the barrel.

I snatched up a scrap of cod and was half way back to the cave when the flock let out a great squawk and I felt wings in my face. One of the feathered devils speared into my paw and robbed me of the fishy treat.

I was driven back to the cave-mouth by a forest of angry beaks. As I slank inside, I noticed that Arnuf was busy with some reeds and sticks that he'd found on the cave floor.

'I'm knitting a gull trap,' he said triumphantly.

'But Arnuf,' I spluttered. 'There are hundreds of flapping fiends in that hell-flock. We'll be cold in our death-mounds by the time you've knitted enough traps to catch them.'

Arnuf put down his basket and looked at me.

'What should we do then?' he asked.

'How should I know?' I moaned. 'Is this is it? Am I to end my days – starving in a dirt-hole – penned in by the beaks of a flock of fish-snatchers?'

On hearing this, Billi rose up and trotted over towards the back of the cave.

'Dinnae fret. Those birds are nae bother,' he said.

With a warlike bleat, he charged at speed with his head down and his horns aimed at the feathered-foe. The flock parted like cloud-mist on a summer morn but they soon wheeled and began to regroup, ready to mob him. However, before they could swoop back and give him a beaking, the little goat raced over and butted the fish barrel into the river. It span about for a moment and then began to float off downstream, with the feathered fiends flying after it.

'See?' said Billi, trotting back to join us. 'I told ye it'd be nae bother.'

'Nae bother!' I moaned. 'You great gull-butting horn-head! What about my fish barrel? Now the only food for a hundred miles is floating down the river.'

I was so furious now that I no longer felt hungry. The threat of the angry birds had gone but also my prize had been carried away by the icy waters.

Then I heard a terrible squawk. One of the birds, and it must have been a particularly stupid one, had somehow managed to climb inside Arnuf's trap.

'Isn't she pretty,' cooed Arnuf. 'Let's call her Valki.'

'Why by Thor's bash-stick do you want to call it that?'

'Because she's a great swooper – just like the Valkeries in the song, old whathisname used to sing us.'

I realised that he was talking about the sagas that his Skald used to sing by the longfire in the great hall of King Ruffgar back in Gutland.

'Arnuf,' I began. 'Do you know what the Valkeries in the sagas used to swoop down for?'

He turned his head to the side and thought hard.

'Er – seedcake?' he suggested.

'The dead – you limp-wit. Valkeries fly down and collect the bodies of the slain heroes.'

Arnuf looked puzzled.

'What do they do that for?'

'They tak them away tae a feast hall in the sky called Valhalla,' bleated Billi.

'Arnuf,' I laughed. 'This is a new low. You have less learning than a half-grown mountain goat.'

'I must have dozed off during that bit,' he said.

Arnuf poked his nose closer to the basket.

'I like Valki,' he announced. 'It's a good name for a gull. And she likes it too – don't you Valki?'

Arnuf picked a worm out of the dirt and threw it into Valki's basket. The winged fiend pecked it in half and tried to swallow but then let out a croaking cough.

'What's the matter Valki?' 'Don't you like wormies?' he cooed.

I trotted over to inspect the trap.

'That gull, has hurt her gullet,' I announced. 'She cannot feed herself. So she will not survive.'

Arnuf dangled another worm at her but the unlucky bird left it unpecked on the floor of the trap.

I stuck a paw inside the cage, seized the flapping seagull by the neck and began to squeeze.

'No!' cried Arnuf, trying to pull the bird away.

'I have never been hungrier,' I growled. I got ready for a neck bite but the bird would not stop flapping. My paws slid off her gullet and she flew to the corner.

'Stop! I beg you!' yelled Arnuf.

'Never!' I screamed. 'I'll feast on seagull and you can find your own dinner. You're worse than the monks.'

'No! Not Valki!' he howled, putting himself between me and the bird. 'Maybe the monks have got a point... about not eating meat I mean...' he pleaded.

'Those prattling prayer-sayers?' I laughed. 'So that's where all this meatless-talk is coming from. Call yourself a war-dog? You'll turn cat-licker next.'

The unfortunate bird was flapping in fury, trying to fly out of the cave. But it kept bouncing off the walls.

'Beowuff! cried Arnuf. 'Beware!'

I cornered the gull and got my paw over its neck.

'Now Arnuf,' I explained. 'Can you not see that we dogs were put here to eat whatever we like. Gulls and goats included. The bigger animals were born to play tyrant to the lesser. The cat rules the mouse. The dog Lords it over the cat. That is the way of things, the ancient law.'

The seagull squawked and pecked me on the nose.

'Beowuff!' howled Arnuf again, pointing over my shoulder towards the back of the cave.

'What?' I snapped. 'I suppose there is a stone-troll or a soil-dwarf behind me? Well that old boar-wash will not work. I was not born yesterday.'

At that moment, there came a scraping noise from the back of the cave. As I span around to face it, a bellowing roar bounced off the walls.

The dark space at the far end of the cave was filled with a musky scent and a huge bristling shape reared up and came rushing at me. I felt a leak run down the back of my leg. In terror, I sprang for the entrance, scrambling over Arnuf on my way to escape the bear that was lumbering towards me, snarling from the back of its grizzled maw. The stench was awful, for the beast's coat was rotten and caked in filth and it was dragging an iron chain behind it. Mange was its only friend.

'Help! Get away!' I whimpered.

'Beowuff,' began Arnuf. 'Is this what you meant when you said that the big animals always play tyrant to the small ones?'

The mountainous bear came lumbering towards me. I backed up but tripped over a wooden post and fell headfirst into the dirt.

'He likes you!' said Arnuf. 'Let's call him Balder.'

'Freya's braids! Why call him that?' I asked.

'Because he's bald, and he's a bear,' answered Arnuf.

'Good. Let's change your name to Salli Slackwit while we are at it,' I growled.

I willed my legs to run, but the leash of fear held me

fast. 'Arnuf!!! Help me!' I cried.

As the mangy demon came closer, it let out a growl. As it roared, it bared its fangs and I caught sight of rows of yellow teeth, sharp as a head-taker's axe.

I was doomed, just as surely as if the goddess Hel had sat me on her sick bed for a little lie down.

The bear gaped at me, opened its jaws wide and shook its great head. Then I noticed that it had a chain and a lock around its neck. For only the second time in my life, I did something that the Skalds would consider to be brave. I thrust my paw into my loot-sack, grabbed the golden key and jammed it into the lock. With a desperate twist I managed to unlock the bear's collar before the beast shook me off. I thought it would bite me in two for the sport of it, but instead the brown brute gave a roar of triumph. It shook off its rust-clad collar and the iron chain fell upon the stones with a crash. Howling for freedom, it turned and charged off.

'Balder! Come back boy!' called Arnuf.

A few hours later, it did return – with its patchy muzzle all covered in fish juice and slew. Arnuf was so delighted that he danced in celebration. To my amazement, the creature lay down beside me like a grateful Carl in front of his Lord's long-fire.

Speaking of fire, for the first time in many nights, we had the comfort of a blaze. The banks of the stream were strewn with driftwood and soon we had collected a good stack of it and piled it up against the stake post. I looked forward to my warmest night in weeks.

Chapter Twelve

Half Mast

The driftwood was wet and the flames were slow to take hold. As the fire struggled and hissed, I watched the white smoke rising.

'I've been thinking Arnuf, why would anyone chain up this mange-pelted growler?' I asked.

'Balder, you mean?' he said in an injured tone.

'Thor's Jaws! Balder then, if you insist. Why would anyone chain a bear to a post and leave it to starve in the middle of nowhere?'

'Leave 'him' to starve don't you mean?' protested Arnuf. 'Balder is a he-bear.'

'Is he really?' I sighed.

'He certainly is. I've seen his under-parts,' said Arnuf.

There was no sane reply to this, so I didn't answer. Instead, I gazed into the smoke as it twisted around the logs. Then I sprang up, tripping over the gull-basket and trampling on the sleeping goat in my excitement.

'What are ye doing?' bleated Billi angrily.

'Digging,' I cried. 'Arnuf, help me!'

'Why are we digging?' he asked, joining me.

'That bear was put here to guard something,' I said.

'But there's nothing here to guard – just a stake-post,' said Arnuf.

'That is not a post, my slow-kenning friend. That is a mast.'

109

Arnuf is not a quick thinker, but he is an amazing digger. So he dug for a while before asking:

'If it's a mast. Where's the ship?'

'Attached to the mast,' I explained.

Arnuf's face twisted in wonder.

'He means under the groond,' explained the goat helpfully.

'There's probably a great chief and all his war-pack buried down there,' I said. 'Along with all manner of loot.'

Arnuf stopped digging and his face sank quicker than a prisoner in a peat bog.

'Don't worry,' I said. 'They'll all be dead and gone. This is a ship-burial.'

'Why would anyone want to be buried in a ship?' whimpered Arnuf, clutching at his cross-sticks.

'Stone me like a crow if I know!' I answered. 'Maybe his war-pack wanted a change from death mounds? Now be silent and dig.'

Arnuf dug deeper and deeper, making a pile of sand and earth alongside the mast.

I would have joined him in the hole but I don't like getting my paws dirty.

He followed the mast down until at last he called up, saying that he had hit something soft.

'I expect it's a sail,' I explained. 'They often covered up the treasure with the ship's sail. Can you cut through it?'

After a long pause for thought, he called back:

'I don't have a knife.'

'Then bite through it,' I ordered.

Now if you are wondering why my mind had turned from my pleading belly to the thought of plunder and loot, then that is a good question.

I had heard about these buried ships from a Dane called Bolvar – we met on a slave deck, if my memory serves. Well, that Danelander swore that the kings of old would bury all manner of things to take to the next world. Including casks of mead and barrels of salt-pork. I was hoping that my weak-witted friend might find a store of such fancies and treats in the dark hole.

'I've bitten through it,' he called. 'Can I come back up now?'

'Have a good sniff of that sail first,' I replied. 'Can you smell anything?

'Yes,' he answered.

'What?'

'A sail.'

'Anything else?' I demanded.

There was a shuffling noise as Arnuf wriggled under the canvas. Then I heard an excited bark.

'There's a store of food down here,' he cried. 'Sacks and sacks of it!'

'Thank the Bearded Bonefather for that!' I yapped, leaping about in excitement, all slobber-mouthed at the thought of a feast.

Then I heard Arnuf howl in despair.

'It's all rotten.'

'What?' I raged. 'Surely there must be something toothsome down there?'

'Wait!' called Arnuf. 'There is one sack that has been preserved.'

'Thank Frey for that,' I exclaimed. 'What's inside it?'

'Salt,' he answered.

Well, I could have stuck a short-sword a long way down his throat. I was just about to climb down when he called up to me.

'I can see a barrel.'

'A barrel? What's inside it?'

'Mead, I think. Urrrrgh! I'm afraid it's no good.'

'Hel's plate! What's the matter this time?'

I have sat next to Arnuf on many a bench. I've watched him eat piles of reeking road-scrape and the sort of stinky leavings that would send a wild-boar rooting for its tusk-brush. But a moan of disappointment rose up from the hole.

'It smells a bit meaty,' he moaned.

'Meaty?' I raged. 'What's wrong with meat?'

'Well – it's just that... back at the monastery, the Abbot told me that eating meat is... like murder.'

'Murder?' I howled. 'I'll give you worse than murder. I'll start brewing Arnuf blood-mead if you don't send that barrel up here right now. Murder indeed! It is I who am dying – for a meat-drink.'

There was a long pause and I think I heard the muttering of prayers and the clattering of his cross-sticks before at last he answered.

'I can't lift the barrel. It's too heavy.'

I should have dropped a rock on him but I threw the chain down instead.

'Fill your waterskin from the barrel and then tie it to this chain,' I demanded. 'I'll haul it up.'

Arnuf is not much of a knot-tier. My belly roared and rumbled. At last, I could stand it no more and I jumped down into the pit and snatched the waterskin from his shaking paw. I took a long pull and gulped down the meat-juice until my gut-sack was full to bursting point.

'Best mead I've ever supped,' I sighed, patting my belly. You should try it. It tastes gamey... with another flavour in there too. Bacon, if I'm not mistaken.'

A crazed look came over my bench-mate's eyes when he heard that word.

'Bacon!!!' he howled, braying like a mule in a barn-fire.

'Aaarrgh! I cannot stand it! Give me that!' he roared.

With that cry, he snatched the vessel from my grip and took a long, steady gulp.

When he'd had his fill, he raised his snout to the glorious light that was streaming down into the hole.

Arnuf's face wobbled and took on an unusual glow.

'If we were not meant to eat animals, how come so many of them are made out of meat?' he moaned.

I gaped in wonder. It was the most sensible thing I'd ever heard Arnuf say. I was about to congratulate him when all manner of weirdness began to dance before my eyes. Sights so strange, that no two peep-holes have seen the like in Utgard, Mitgard or mighty Asgard itself.

'Rabbits!' cried Arnuf. 'Rabbits everywhere!'

I could not take my eyes off my bench-mate.

'Beowuff, it's the Hiddenfolk. I've always wanted to meet them,' he laughed.

At the top of the shaft I heard a roar of alarm. I craned my neck upwards to see the bear rearing up on its hind legs and bellowing. Then I blinked in wonder. For his ragged fur had dropped away. His mangy coat rippled and turned into gleaming fur. His proud eyes shone brightly. His wise head was crowned with silver. Beside him stood a goat with its horns aflame. It called to me – but its bleats were now deep as a boom-horn. I wanted to listen, but Arnuf's voice was still raving.

'Rabbits!' he cried. 'The pink rabbits are coming.'

With a great effort, I twisted my snout towards the voice. The next thing I saw sent tear-floods running from my amazed eyes.

My weak-witted bench-mate stood before me. But he was dressed like a Sea-King of old – with a silver brooch, fine robes and a broadsword hanging from a silver belt.

I could only point and stare and babble. I felt the urge to fall to the ground before him, ready to receive the wisdom of the long-fathers from this sage-king.

'Beowuff!' he laughed, 'Look at yourself in that get-up!'

I tried to answer but I could not speak.

'Stop it! You're giving me gut-ache,' he giggled, offering me the mead once again. 'Want some more?' he laughed, throwing the waterskin towards me.

I willed my paws to catch it but it hit me hard in the face. When I looked again, he was still holding it in his shaking paw. Then I realised what was happening.

'Arnuf!' I cried. 'The mead... Don't drink it... There's something wrong with the mead... Give me that!'

Arnuf threw it over and I pulled out the stopper, tipping the sweet liquid onto the dirt. At last, I found what I was looking for: there were fleshy strips at the bottom of the waterskin.

'Recognise these?' I asked.

'That's my ground meat,' said Arnuf.

'Ground meat?' I growled. 'You mean the Hel's caps? You were storing them – in our waterskin?'

Some time later, we lay around a roaring fire, recovering our muddled wits.

'You should have seen yourself Beowuff – you were a sight for the Skald's to sing about,' said Arnuf.

On most days I would have slapped him on the snout-hole for storing toadstools in one of our empty waterskins. I had made him turn them out of the food-sack you see, but later he had sneaked back and saved them. I should have bashed him roundly on the brain-case. But I had supped a lot of the toadstool-laced mead, and in truth, I found the whole adventure very funny.

The goat had come to our rescue and pulled us out

of the hole. Then he gave us something to make us sick. I do not know how he managed this. It takes a lot to make Arnuf sick. Perhaps it was salt water?

The sweats and the sickness were almost gone now and the two of us sat shivering by a driftwood fire.

'You were a pretty sight!' said Arnuf again.

'Whatdoyoumean!!!' I spluttered, splashing cold river water onto my nose. 'It can't have been that bad. Did I have two heads? Or eight legs like Bodin's horse?'

'It was worse!' he insisted. 'You were all dressed up,' he began. 'No I cannot tell...'

'Dressed up as what?' I asked.

'No! I cannot say it,' giggled Arnuf.

'Out with it!' I demanded, fearing he'd reveal that I was painted like a Swedish she-dog.

'Go on,' I said. 'Tell me. I will not bite.'

'You were dressed,' said Arnuf. 'Like a m...'

'Like what? Like a moon-cow? Like a muck-sniffer?'

'Like a monk,' he declared. 'Like a Brother from Sine Carne.'

But before I could answer, Valki let out a squawk of alarm and took off in a hurry. The goat began to bleat in terror.

'Billi? What's the matter?' I called.

I staggered up as best as I could but then I buckled like a cheap Swedish floor.

'Raiders!' he cried, taking to his heels and racing away down the beach. 'Gang on! Run fer it!'

CHAPTER THIRTEEN

THE HAGSMOUTH

Alas, Arnuf and I were in no fit state to 'gang' anywhere. At his best my bench-mate is war-shy. But when confronted by the attackers he came over all leak-legged. He didn't even try to run. He just sat quivering in a heap, clutching his cross-sticks and howling like a harpooned seal.

The raiding party soon had us in slave-boots and marched us off with a clank.

Although we didn't know it, we were not far from the sea. The gorge we'd been following ended at the foot of a wide estuary. Soon I could make out white capped breakers in the distance.

It was a hard walk to their longboat, and as we tramped, Fear and her best friend Regret played with my mead-muddled mind.

Arnuf's first thoughts were for his 'friends' by which he meant the Billi and Balder. Our enemies had got the goat. He'd run straight into a cage. Somehow they'd driven the bear into a ravine and got a rope around his neck. Only Valki managed to fly to safety. How I envied that gull. To be able to fly off and carry yourself high out of harm's reach. What a shame that I'd been born with legs rather than wings to flee with.

The sun was dipping as we got to their longboat. Two rag-eared war-dogs stood guard as we approached.

The first had a typically cruel look about him, as if his heart was pumping poison round his veins. His mate was a big mastiff with a lolling tongue and eyes that were warmer, which is not to say that they were particularly kind.

'Wait!' I began. 'My friends, I fear that there has been a terrible mistake...'

The cruel one's eyes didn't even flicker. He'd done a lot of slaving by the look of him – and I expect he had heard every sob story under the wicked moon.

The mastiff turned towards me, and I took this for a sign to carry on begging.

'Good shore-guards,' I began. 'Have a heart...'

The second war-dog growled and flashed his fangs. I saw that the fashion for tooth-filing had made its way this far north. His teeth were as sharp as a new set of meat-knives.

'We are far from home,' I whined. 'Two travellers, a drain-maker and a Skald. We were shipwrecked...'

When the mastiff hear the word 'Skald' he let out an excited bark and loosened his hold on our chains.

'A Skald? Did you say?' he growled, in the Gutland tongue, or something very like it.

'That's right,' I said brightly. 'A master of sagas.'

'A Skald eh?' said the mastiff, turning towards his point-toothed mate. He yanked Arnuf's chain and sniffed hard, as if he had the scent of a lie.

Arnuf nodded and wagged his tail. The guard bit it.

'Untie the Skald,' ordered the cruel one. 'Send the

drain-maker down the whale-road.'

As I heard this, my heart grew as cold as ice-water.

'Which is which?' demanded the mastiff.

I let them argue for a while and when their talk finally ran into a pool of silence, I dived in.

'I'm the Skald.' I said. 'I'll come with you.'

The mastiff looked puzzled.

'You said you were a muck-raker!' he snapped.

'Drain-maker, do you mean?' 'That's Arnuf over there. Sniff him if you don't believe me, he still has the reek of sewer-holes on him.'

'Don't worry! He'll get a good scrubbing where he's going,' laughed the file-tooth. 'The Hagsmouth licks everything clean.'

He jumped up, pawing at his mate. I joined in the mocking laughter as loud as I dared.

'You've heard of the Hagsmouth then?' he asked.

'Something of it,' I muttered, after a long pause.

'There!' he snarled, pointing at a line of rocks.

We were steering a careful course alongside a spine of black crags that stuck up out of the water like the bristles on a boar's back. In the middle of the reef was a gap, like a gaping mouth.

'The Hagsmouth,' laughed my captor. 'Where the water-witch lives. Whatever gets sucked into her jaws, never comes out, be it a warship or a winkle-boat.'

I peered across the black water and followed his paw towards a line of rocks, but there was no sign of a whirlpool.

The mastiff grabbed Arnuf's chain and dragged him howling towards the side of the boat.

'You stink,' laughed the war-dog, sticking his nose close to Arnuf's. 'The Hagsmouth will wash the sewer-stench off you, you filthy little runt.'

I watched them haul my meak-mawed bench-mate over towards the rail. There was a lot of howling as Arnuf was dangled overboard, followed by a muffled bark and then a loud splash.

When it was over, the mastiff trotted back to the lurcher's side.

I felt a cold panic, deep in my gut-sack. Arnuf was a ditch-licker, but he did not deserve to die like this.

'Fourteen years...' I muttered.

'Old bench-mate of yours?' asked the lurcher.

'Fear not, for you'll join him soon,' said the mastiff.

'Fourteen years,' I sighed. 'Forty two Swedish sagas...'

'Sagas?' barked the lurcher in a fury, sniffing at the deck where Arnuf had just stood. 'But... you... you said that you were the Skald and he was the drain-Lord.'

'I am a Skald,' I answered. 'Rules are rules. You need to know fifty sagas, before you can call yourself a Skald. Poor Arnuf only knows forty two.'

The war-dogs looked at each other.

'Forty two stories?' yapped the lurcher. 'If the Half-Dragon hears of this, he'll tear our tongues out.'

'Rope!' cried the mastiff, rushing over to the rail. 'Shut yer snout-hole and throw him a line before the Hagsmouth takes him!'

Chapter Fourteen

The Half-Dragon

Poor Arnuf sat dripping on the boards, clutching at his cross-sticks in a panic.

'A dragon!!!' he howled.

'He's only a dog,' I whispered. 'Listen carefully, if you want to live. The King of the Dragon raiders is known in their clan by the title of "Dragon-Lord" and his sons are called the Half-Dragons. And the son of the Half-Dragon is called the Quarter-Dragon and so on.'

'Four dragons!' cried Arnuf. 'Saints protect us!'

For a moment, I wished I hadn't talked the raiders into hauling Arnuf back aboard. But my weak-witted bench-mate was reeling from the shock of his recent soaking, so I did not correct him and explain that there was in fact only one Half-Dragon at this present time. Our captor had put all of his Brothers to the sword. Why would a Half-Dragon want to murder his Brothers in cold blood? So that he could become the Dragon-Lord without a challenge, of course! If this sounds harsh, consider that they would most likely have done the same to him, or worse.

'Listen Arnuf, we only have to worry about the Half-Dragon,' I explained.

'What does he want from us?' asked Arnuf.

'Stories,' I replied.

'Why does he want stories?' asked my bewildered bench-mate.

I did not know the answer. That very question had kept me awake for long hours in the bilge hole where we were now imprisoned.

'Perhaps he likes a good tale? I expect he gets lonely in his cave at night, sitting on top of that gold heap.'

'The Half-Dragon does not sleep in a cave,' I sighed. 'If you want to keep a tongue in your mouth then choose your words with care when he sends for you.'

Arnuf sat biting at his cross-sticks. I decided to lick them for good luck. I needed all the good fortune I could get.

I drifted into a troubled sleep which was soon shattered by a bark.

'Shift it, you sea-snots!' bellowed a grim voice. 'Leap when your Liege-Lord orders it!'

'Here they are Fangar,' said the lurcher with the filed teeth, unlocking the cage with a quivering paw.

I recognised Fangar from the chronicle house. Thankfully he did not remember my face or he would have skinned me on the spot. He was the Half-Dragon's eyes, ears and jaws. He had been given the title 'Jarl' – which is usually as high up the Thane ladder as you can climb before the rungs get blood-soaked.

Fangar was taking us for a private audience with his Lord. On the way to the chamber he explained that few had met his master and lived.

At the head of a finely carved table, sat the Half-Dragon. He was very old and thoroughly wicked.

He beckoned to us to approach. As I drew closer, I noticed the carvings on his high-seat. A winged dragon, grinning cruelly as it sat on top of a skull-pile.

I looked into his eyes and tried not to shudder. Surely this death-bringer was after more than a few stories?

'Are these the Skalds?' he asked softly.

'Aye Lord!' boomed Fangar. 'One fully trained, and the other with forty two tales to his name.'

'Let them approach,' he whispered.

Fangar yanked at my chain and dragged me by the collar till my nose was level with his master's claws. They were yellowing and cracked with age.

'You know fifty sagas?' he asked.

I could only nod and pray that Arnuf kept a hold of his tongue. 'From which lands do these tales come?'

'From far over the whale-road, where only Sleipnir can tread,' I said. 'From the distant lands of the Fins and the Danes.'

He let out a snort, and seemed happy with this.

'How about you?' he whispered, turning to Arnuf. 'Where do your sagas come from?'

I turned towards Arnuf, willing him to speak. If he did not answer, he would surely die.

'Icelandland,' he whimpered.

I prayed that he would not go leak-legged on me.

The Half-Dragon frowned.

'He means Iceland, Lord,' I muttered.

'In the songs of these lands, have you ever heard tell of a thing called a Wain stone, or a Sarcen stone, or a Star Stone?' he asked.

I felt a blood-rush and my heart hammered in my chest. I did not know what answer to give him.

If I answered him 'nay', I'd soon be kissing the Hagsmouth, or worse. But if I told him that I'd heard of it, he would not just thank me and let me walk free! For once, old Beowuffer did not know what to say.

'Speak,' said the old Dragon, 'Do not try to hide what you know.'

'Others who held their tongues were begging to keep hold of them later,' laughed Fangar.

I had a feeling that he was a tongue-taker.

'I know what it is to be a vow breaker. So you can nod if you know the thing I am speaking of,' hissed the old Dragon.

I felt myself nod and then bowed my head again.

The Half-Dragon smiled.

'Why do you seek for this Star Stone?' I asked, not knowing where the words had come from.

'For many years, our Dragon-clan has drifted over the seas. Only the stone can guide us back to the land of our long-fathers. Do any of your sagas tell of this?' he asked.

'Only one that I know,' I answered softly.

I looked at Arnuf and then at Fangar.

'Forgive me Lord, I will tell it. But the words of the tale are for the ears of Lords and Lords alone...'

'Lords' ears!' growled Fangar in a fury.

'Leave us!' hissed the Half-Dragon, sending Fangar and my bench-mate running from the chamber with the wave of his ancient paw.

CHAPTER FIFTEEN

A FLEET OF TROUBLES

The wind on deck was biting, but at least we were out of the bilge hole.

'Beowuff? You are safe!' cried Arnuf. 'I feared that the Dragon-Lord had burned you to blazes.'

'Not yet,' I muttered. 'But he will if I don't find him a Star Stone.'

Arnuf looked at me and began to whimper.

'What about our friends?' he said.

I didn't know what he was talking about, so I made no answer.

'Billi, Balder and Valki. Did you save their lives too?' he asked.

'Er... yes,' I answered, I suppose I did. 'Valki flapped off, so you need not worry about her.'

'Thank the Saints for that,' said Arnuf.

After a cold night on deck with nothing to eat but hard biscuits, the wind finally dropped. The next morning, I lay in the sunshine as a fleet of troubled thoughts sailed through my head.

'Beowuff!' cried Arnuf in excitement. 'Land! I think I can see the land!'

As he danced about in excitement, skipping around the deck, I lay perfectly still.

'Wake me up when you're sure,' I growled.

'How can I be sure?' he asked.

'If it's land, it'll be dry,' I answered.

Later, he began to squeal like a pig in a thorn bush.

'Beowuff! Wake up! Make haste! It is land!' he called. 'And we've been here before.'

'Don't be a slack-wit,' I said. 'Have you taken another bash on the brain-case?'

He leapt to the rail, his hackles bristling.

'We're back! At the monastery!' he cried.

'Really?' I replied, trying to sound surprised.

But my bench-mate got the scent of a lie.

'Beowuff?' he began. 'You knew we were coming back, didn't you?'

'What if I did?' I snarled.

'Beowuff!' howled my bench-mate. 'How could you? You said you'd help the Brothers and the old monk-father. But now you've returned with their enemies.'

'How do you think I saved you from old fire-fangs back there?' I growled. 'He was about to send both of us down the Hagspout in a holed-bucket. He wants news of this Star Stone, so I had to tell him something.'

'But...! Why? Why did you tell them it was at the monastery?' he stammered.

After another long pause, a smile spread across his gormless snout-hole. He pressed his nose close to mine and winked at me.

'Say no more,' he laughed. His tail began to thump against the boards. 'This is one of your tricks, isn't it? To save the Brothers. You're planning something.'

I winked back at him. It took a lot to shake Arnuf's

trust in me. It lasted as the raiders moored their long-boat in that gentle bay. It even lasted when Fangar told Arnuf that he was to be held on the Dragon's ship, as a pledge of my promise to bring back the Star Stone from Sin Carne. Fangar's pack made it clear as spring water that if I was not back by noon, they would personally send Arnuf down the sea-witch's sink-hole.

Arnuf still wasn't worried. I was waving goodbye when a growl shook the ship. Two of Fangar's Thanes were unloading our bear. The bald brute caught one of them with a paw-swipe and made him squeal like a kitten.

'Gerrofff me! You manky monster!' barked the startled Dragon raider, howling in pain and clutching at his side. 'We'll light a pretty fire that keeps your toes warm tonight.'

'Beowuff!' called Arnuf. 'You promised you'd save them! They are our companions on the quest.'

'He did save 'em,' laughed the Dragon wheeling the cage up the beach. 'For a sacrifice.'

'Nooooo!' cried Arnuf.

I did not answer. I simply trudged off up the beach in the direction of the causeway.

Now, the Beowuffer of old would have given the Dragon raiders his thanks – trotted off towards the monastery and then as soon as he was out of sight, turned tail and run for his life. However there was the small matter of my weak-witted friend. Much as it was tempting, I could not bear to let them send him down the Hagsmouth. He didn't deserve to be whirled to death in that hell-pool. What is more, the Half-Dragon was keeping an evil eye on me. He had sent a couple of spies to follow me up the beach. So I was trapped like a gull in a gutting shed. If I wasn't back with the Star Stone by nightfall, they'd put the monastery to the torch, and use my tail to guide them towards the torchholder! If I tried to sneak off, I'd be tracked and taken. Worst of all, there was no Star Stone anyway. So I'd have to find something inside that miserable monk-hole that would pass for a magical rune-stone. No wonder I was grumbling as I trudged along the causeway.

When the Brothers opened their gates I was met by young Fastwagger.

'Beowuff! You are back!' he barked. 'May all the Saints be praised!'

I thought he was going to weep at the sight of me. 'We monks sometimes say that "He works in mysterious ways" and so it has been proved this time!'

He was about to find out exactly how mysterious.

'Stop prayer-prattling,' I barked. 'Take me to the Abbot. I have news that cannot wait.'

'To the Abbot? Of course,' he yapped. 'The Thing is in session. The Brothers are in the Uttery. Follow me.'

The bear and the goat were put on leashes and brought behind me. Billi was angry. His voice was cracked after long hours of bleating for help. But he was relieved to be out of his cage. I decided to put a muzzle around him to stop him from blabbing to the Brothers.

That old growler Balder was the problem. He was all set to play havoc but Brother Sagus softened his rage with a stack of honeycombs. Honey you see is the secret ingredient of their meatless mead. The monks kept bee hives in their garden. Soon the bear was following him about like a lap-dog.

As I entered the Uttery, I was hailed by a familiar voice.

'Beowuff! So you return at last. And you've brought some storm clouds with you, I see.'

It was that saxe-faced snour-snout Hardlarder.

He hadn't become any cheerier whilst I'd been on my travels.

'Where is Abbot Goodoldboyson? I have important tidings that he must hear this very minute,' I blustered.

'Goodoldboyson? He is busy in the fields. On a task of great importance,' growled Hardlarder.

'What? What's he doing there?' I asked.

'Enlarging the sewer,' said Fastwagger. 'He has undertaken to dig it out with his bare paws. He says that it will help make up for his sins...'

'Have the autumn storms whipped through his brain-case and swept away his wits?' I cried. 'The enemy are headed towards his monastery, and the Abbot is busy digging ditches!'

Hardlarder let out a little cough.

'I am Abbot now,' he announced.

I could not believe this news. I had left the place under the charge of the friendly old Goodoldboyson but returned to find that somehow Hardlarder had got himself appointed monk-father in chief! The old sour-puss was as sharp as a Dragon's scale and he was taking pleasure in my astonishment.

'You are the new Abbot?' I stammered. 'What a blessing for the monastery. May I be the first to congratulate you Brother?'

'No,' growled Hardlarder. 'You may not.'

He looked at me in the same way that a heron looks at a stickleback before beaking it to pieces and devouring it.

'The old Abbot trusted you with an important mission,' he began, shaking in rage. 'And what heroes have you brought us? A bear with no hair. And a goat with a sore throat?'

I stood for some moments thinking up a reply.

'We also have a gull with a stuck gullet,' I added, 'but she flew off.'

'Fine heroes these!' raged Abbot Hardlarder, his hackles rising. 'You will get nothing from us – nothing but scorn – and a heartfelt prayer that He commands your tongue to stop twisting the truth each time you open your lying maw.'

The bear, who did not like being shouted at any more than I do, got up and let out a great rumbling grunt of disapproval.

'Take that flea ridden monster with you. Heroes indeed!' scoffed Hardlarder.

'That's Balder,' I explained. 'He used to belong to a

Berserker. They shaved him to make their bear-shirts for battle. That's how he lost his coat...'

Hardlarder stood stone-faced and made no answer. I could not tell what he made of my tale.

'Impressed?' I said cheerily. 'You should be giving thanks Brothers. For this is not just any goat. This is Thor's own goat – Ragnar – who cannot die. Why I have seen him cheat death by hanging, drowning, fire and rockfall.'

A gasp went up around the room.

'Now I'm getting through to them,' I thought. Old Beowuffer could talk a snail out of its own shell.

Hardlarder sat gaping – open mawed. So I carried on with my stream of nonsense.

'The gull that went missing is a Firebird – shield maiden to Bodin the Bearded Bonefather no less.'

There was another gasp of astonishment.

Hardlarder began to cough. At first I thought he was ill but then he opened his mouth and roared.

'Thor? Bodin? How dare you speak the names of Heathens in the His House?'

'He meant no harm Abbot...' began Fastwagger.

'Silence! Blasphemy!' cried the new Abbot, with the bone of my error clamped firmly between his teeth.

'Perhaps we should hear his tidings first?' suggested Fastwagger.

But the old joy-killer was having none of it.

'Go!' he growled. 'Be gone. I banish you. Never darken this hall again!'

I knew it was no use, but I made one last appeal as I backed out of his hall.

'Er, fine,' I called. 'But do you want the heroes? I could do you a good deal on the bear and the goat…'

'Your lying tongue would try the patience of a saint,' growled Hardlarder. 'Now leave us before I break my vow and strike you down myself!'

'By the way,' I replied, with just a hint of a sneer in my voice. 'Your friends the Dragons are back – they're waiting in the bay. I'd be surprised if they don't sack this place before nightfall. I'd stay and help you with the chanting if it wasn't for this lying tongue of mine. I fear it makes prayer-words stick in my throat.'

Fastwagger sprang to his feet.

'Beowuff! Wait!' he called.

But I didn't wait. Leading the bear behind me, I ran off through the tunnels. I decided to head for the gates and run from that unhappy monk-hole as fast as my fleeing legs would carry me.

I later learned that The Monks of Sine Carne had never turned away anyone from their monastery before they gave me my marching orders. There's a first time for everything – I was almost proud.

My plan to sell 'heroes' to the monks was in tatters, so there was no point in dragging Balder along. Cursing, I threw down his rope and ran down the corridor.

I was surprised to find myself standing beside Brewboiler, the monks' great mead-kettle. Fastwagger must have got the Dragons to return it. Pausing to catch my breath, I had a sudden change of heart and went back to take the muzzle off Balder. The thought of a starving bear on the loose brought a smile to my lips. It would surely strike fear into the hearts of those muttering meak-wits.

The great bear-mountain sat patiently whilst I removed the rope. The muscles on his flanks were enormous. Sadly, bear is said to be the least toothsome of meats.

Once his face was free of the muzzle, Balder let out a triumphant yowl – bears are supposed to like caves so I expect he liked it in these mouldy old monk-tunnels. Licking my lips I looked at my young friend Billi (or Ragnar as I'd just called him in front of the monks). He would be a far more useful travelling companion since goat flesh can be cut up and dried in meaty strips. Sadly I had no time for skinning and curing him, so I decided that I'd better set him free as well.

'Thank ye Beowuff! For a while I thought ye were out tae rook me, but yer alright,' he called as he ran off down the tunnel. 'I'll nae forget this.'

Thinking about cured goat-meat had set my belly churning once again. I dug down into my loot-sack but it was empty save for a couple of book clasps. Cursing, I pulled out a waterskin. I was about to drink but then I remembered that there was still toadstool juice in there. I didn't want to be hopping about the halls talking to pink bunnies again, so I spat it out immediately.

I was about to throw it away but then a thought entered into my head and a smile came to my lips. I decided to empty the toadstool-juice into Brewboiler. That would give those pious prattlers something to pray about! I imagined their faces when they started seeing pink bunnies hopping around their prayer-halls.

In a flash I was up the ladder and I had the lid off the great kettle. The smell of honeyed mead flew into my nostrils and set my guts quivering.

Then I thought of that sour-faced hound Hardlarder. becoming the new Abbot. What a curse-stroke! Reaching into my loot-sack, I took out the rest of the Helscaps and threw them in. The sickly smell from the toadstools filled the air.

As they sank down into the mead-kettle, a sudden bark surprised me and I nearly fell off the ladder.

'Beowuff,' called Fastwagger. 'Thank goodness I've found you.'

I slid casually down the ladder, trying to act innocent. I hoped he hadn't seen me fouling his precious brew, but I need not have worried. Brother Fastwagger would not know an evildoer if they bit him on the bottom. And then he'd probably turn the other cheek.

'I was just, er saying a road-prayer at the start of my journey,' I muttered, hiding the golden book clasp that I'd helped myself to on the way here.

The young monk sniffed at me happily and smiled. 'Beowuff. I am sorry. About Abbot Hardlarder, I mean. I know that in your heart, you meant well. You did your best to help us.'

I said nothing, making sure to get my loot-sack

hidden before I turned to face him.

'What do you want?' I asked.

'You've returned alone Beowuff,' he answered. 'Where is your friend Skaldi?'

In truth, I had forgotten about my weak-willed bench-mate. So I decided to make up some nonsense.

'Arnuf you mean? I'm afraid he was – er – lost on the voyage,' I said sadly.

Fastwagger let out a howl of torment.

'Bless him! But fear not – heal your heart – for I know he is in a better place,' he sighed.

If he was talking about the slave-pen of a Dragon longboat then this was a new meaning of the saying 'a better-place'!

I rolled my eyes to the skies and nodded.

'If you really want to help me,' I said, 'Find me a bag of those delicious monk-biscuits.'

Before I'd finished speaking, he produced two bags from under his cloak.

'Take all you need,' he said cheerily. 'It is said that The Lord helps those who help themselves...'

I almost choked on my first mouthful.

'Does He indeed?' I answered, fingering the stolen book-clasps in my loot sack. Perhaps there was more to Him that meets the eye. 'Bless you Brother. Now step aside for I must make haste.'

'Good luck Brother Beowuff!' he called as I made for the light at the end of the monk-tunnel. I was surprised to find myself stopping and looking back.

'Listen Fastwagger – here's a little scrap of learning

for you that you won't find in a monk-chronicle. By sundown the Half-Dragon and his war-pack are going to attack this place – so if I were you, I'd go and join your ex-abbot in the sewer. Keep out of harm's way. If you want my advice, lock those gates of yours and bar them.'

'I cannot,' he said sadly. 'The Abbot has forbidden it. The doors of the Lord's House must always stand open.'

'Lock them Fastwagger,' I begged. 'If anyone makes a fuss, say that you saw it in a vision. And you might start boiling some hot oil in that kettle of yours and take it up to the walls. The only way to repel the Dragons is to burn the thieving coats off their backs. You'll just have to start doing some of the smiting for yourselves.'

As I was talking, he gaped – wide-mawed at me – his tongue lolling out in wonder and shock.

'And I'd stay off the meatless mead too, if I were you,' I said finally. 'There, now I've said it. I don't know why I'm helping you – it's against my way of life.'

We both dashed down the corridor and after a hard run, we reached the open gates. Fastwagger leapt onto the wall and peered out towards the bay. The Dragon ship was nowhere to be seen.

He breathed a sigh of relief and pawed at his cross-sticks, but I wasn't fooled. Fangar and his mates were out there somewhere, skulking just around the head-land. And if I knew the Half-Dragon – they'd already be sharpening their axes and singing their battle-songs.

CHAPTER SIXTEEN

BAD CAUSE

W ell, bench-mates, do you remember that old Beowuffer said earlier that only the weak-witted would set off along a causeway at 'half water'? Yet there I was, with the waves whipping the spray around my trembling paws, preparing to begin my crossing.

It was like this. If I tried to get across the causeway, I would probably drown. But if I stayed with the prayer-sayers, the Half-Dragon would find out that I'd played him false and lied about the Star Stone. Surely my head would take leave of my neck soon afterwards?

My limbs were all a-quiver as I set out along the lonely strand of stones, flanked on both sides by the wild north sea. Then I heard a growl and I nearly slipped off in astonishment. It was Balder, following close behind me. And behind him, came a certain goat.

We'd got half way to the beach when a wave rolled over the stones and I lost sight of the path. I yelled out a stream of curses that could have made the head monk turn heathen. Billi let out a frightened bleat.

'What are we gonna dae Beowuff?' he moaned.

I wondered whether I could use a drowned goat as a float. But to my amazement, the bear went ahead and jumped into the sea. I grabbed the rope that was trailing behind him.

'Swim Balder! Swim!' I called in encouragement.

If only he could tow me to the safety of the shore, I might be saved from the cruel sea.

Balder let out a bellow and began to thrash about with his mighty paws. Then he raised his nose and sniffed the breeze, looking across towards the shore.

I tugged hard on the rope.

'Swim!' I called again. 'Swim you Prince of Bears!'

Balder let out a groan and flailed his paws through the water like cartwheels. This bear was strong enough to uproot an oak. Surely he could drag me across?

With a roar he began to swim – back to the monastery.

'No! No!' I spat. 'You flea-flecked slack-wit! You wave-shy waster! You're going the wrong way!'

All the time I was taking in mouthfuls of salt water.

But that confounded creature had no intention of towing me to the beach. He'd set his heart on returning to Sin Carne. So I was dragged back along the causeway, cursing loudly as the goat paddled along beside me, bleating forlornly.

Bears can look after themselves and there are few safer places for a tender young goat than a meatless-monastery. However, things were looking bleak for Beowuff. I thought about letting go of the rope.

There was nothing to do but wait for my doom. As the darkness gathered, I stood on the wall, watching for a sign. Then, inevitable as the dawn, a tiny light appeared on the horizon. Slowly, it got bigger. I heard a wail behind me, the monks had seen it too. A grim bell began to toll and the monks flung their prayers at the heavens as the Dragon ships sailed towards us.

Well, as you can imagine, the Dragon raiders were a well-drilled crew of throat biters. Before you could shout: 'Pillage at will!' they'd moored their boats and were ready in good raiding order. Their torches were blazing, their thin-lipped axes were ready for chopping. Their swords were as long as lances and as sharp as gutting knives. When the Dragon-pack rushed through the open gates they let out terrible war-cries as the mortified monks fell weeping into the mud, praying for deliverance from the fury of the North Pack.

Not that I actually saw any of this, for at the time I was hiding in an empty mead barrel. But I imagine that it was business as usual.

At last, I gathered enough courage to peep out from my hiding hole. I would have been more than happy to stay put but I heard voices crying for out for monk-mead, so I knew that I had to flee.

When I stuck my head out, I saw a familiar face.

It was Fangar, eying up the keg I'd been hiding in. I thought I was lost but then there came a mighty cheer.

'Who needs barrels when you can sup monk-brew straight from the kettle!' said a happy voice. 'Come on! There's enough mead here to float a longboat!'

Fangar and his pack rushed over to Brewboiler and began to pour the meatless mead down their throats as if Ragnarok itself was about to begin.

'Try it Lord, it's the best drink in the North,' said Fangar.

I allowed myself a sly laugh, remembering the

Helscaps I'd placed in it earlier. Then a growl wiped the smirk off my face.

'Leave that!!' barked a cold voice. I heard the clatter of a drinking horn as it hit the cobble stones.

It was the Half-Dragon himself, come to join the raiding party. Clearly, he was not in the mood for meat-less-mead-tasting.

'Find that rat-wipe Beowuff. He knows where the stone is hidden,' ordered the Dragon Lord.

I was crouching under a sack, cowering like a cat-licker, when I heard a whimper at my side.

'Beowuff!' whispered Fastwagger. 'Thank goodness! You have returned in our hour of need.'

Never mind their hour of need! What about mine?

I had no heart to tell him that his 'miracle' was due to the rising tide on the causeway and a brainless bear.

'What shall we do Beowuff? he asked earnestly.

'Which of the monastery buildings have doors that lock or bar?' I demanded.

Fastwagger thought hard for a moment...

'The new chronicle house has doors that bar, but...'

'Stop yapping!' I ordered. 'If you do not want to meet your maker, lead me to the chronicle house at once.'

I had but one thought, to hide myself behind the strongest doors in the monastery.

Like a good dog, he did exactly as he was told.

Through a rat-run of smaller corridors, he led me to a stone building which stood right at the centre of the unhappy monk-house. It had curious walls with stepped stones that faced in. It looked a little bit like a pine cone laid flat on its side. As Fastwagger had promised – its walls were made of flint and behind its great oak door there was a stout bar set into the wall on iron hinges.

Outside this stronghold I met another familiar face. Clutching an ancient book, wearing a scowl as stoney as his monastery walls, sat Abbot Hardlarder.

I looked past him towards the door of the chronicle house. I was all for leaving him to Fangar's pack, especially after what he'd said to me earlier. But Fastwagger helped the old sour-snout up and I led him inside.

As the door slammed shut, the old sour-snout began to moan and I soon regretted my kindness.

Hardlarder wasn't too stunned to sneer at me.

'Come to marshal your forces have you?' he cried, pointing to the corner. 'It's good to see The Defenders of Sine Carne are here to save us.'

I didn't know what he was babbling about – but then I sniffed the familiar scents of Balder and Billi.

I begged the pair of them to keep quiet.

'Lead us Beowuff. What are we to do?' barked Fastwagger.

He propped the new Abbot against a wall. Hardlarder was shaking and muttering something about the Chronicles of Fidus.

'What should we do Beowuff?' asked Fastwagger.

'I'll give you a commandment,' I snapped.

'What?' he replied.

'Shut your yap before the Fangar's pack hear you.'

But it was too late. As the words left my mouth, I heard iron-clad claws on the cobbles outside. My shore-shy friend Balder let out a low moan, like the rumbling of a giant's gut-sack.

There was a bang on the door – followed by snarling laughter. The oak door was solid enough, but would it hold? I clutched at it like a drowning rat, trying to hope. I even thought about saying a prayer for myself.

Then I felt a chill blast of wind.

The chamber was lit by a pale light. Raising my nose to the heavens, I looked up at the wild moon and spotted three famous ropes of sky-diamonds: Wodin's Wagon, (or was it Bodin's Bear?); Ragnar's horns and another one whose name I've forgotten.

Then I almost howled the stars down from the sky.

'The roof!' I moaned. 'Where's the roof?'

'We haven't finished building it yet,' replied Fastwagger.

'You slack-witted saint-praiser! I told you to take me to the safest place in Sin Carne!' I growled.

Fastwagger shook his head.

'No Beowuff. You asked me which of the monastery's buildings have doors that lock or bar. This chronicle house is the only one with a lock.'

'But there's no roof! You meak-minded mendicant!' I snarled. 'What good is a locked door if the roof gapes wider than Hel's hallway?'

I heard the clatter of more iron-clad claws arriving.

Fastwagger began to pray. Then I heard Hardlarder's dour voice grumbling from behind me.

'Truly it has not happened by chance. Someone has brought this on us. But now, you who are left, stand eagerly, fight bravely, defend the monastery!'

Surely he wasn't expecting me for fight for him?

There was no time to answer. A row of war-dogs appeared, snarling down at us from the gap where the roof should have been.

It is weird what you recall when you are caught in danger's jaws. I remember that the first Dragon raider to leap down was wearing a golden nose-ring.

The second dog to jump down had a familiar face.

'Fangar!!!' I cried. 'By Thor's cloud-thumper! Thank the seven stars you're here.'

I desperately tried to make it look as if I'd been trying to swing the door open.

'Lend a paw with this,' I cried. 'It's stuck like a pebble in a sink-hole.'

Fangar let out an excited bark and joined me at the door. He seemed a little unsteady.

'Paaaahhhh!' he said as he heaved the bar out of its fitting. 'You are weak. They should have named you Beowuff Lady-Paws.'

'Good one Fangar,' I laughed 'Now fetch the Half-Dragon. I have something to show him.'

Fangar wobbled for a moment with his tongue lolling out, then he finally sprang through the door.

'Why not take your war-pack with you?' I suggested.

If I wasn't quaking like a ditch-licker, I would have cheered for joy.

Fangar checked himself and skidded to a halt.

'What has he got for me?' asked a cold voice. 'Has he found what I seek?'

'Yes Lord,' replied Fangar.

Fangar's master had arrived.

'Show me!' demanded the Half-Dragon, stalking into the room with a pack of Thanes at his heels. The place bristled with war-dogs, brandishing axes and knives. Their teeth were filed to points, but I remember thinking that they weren't assembled in the best battle order. The room suddenly stank of monk-mead.

'Look Lord!' gasped Fanger, raising his nose towards the roof-hole and shaking with excitement.

The war-pack followed his gaze.

'The stars!' cried Fangar. 'See how they dance.'

Excited gasps and a number of sworn oaths from the warrior dogs filled the chamber.

The Half-Dragon looked up for what seemed like an age, and when he lowered his long snout down to ground level, there was no wonder in his eyes.

'I see... nothing,' he said slowly.

Fangar's face sunk like a holed longboat. He pitched about, wobbling and spluttering curses.

'What do you mean, nothing?' he asked in amazement. 'Can't you see it?'

The Half-Dragon shook his head. His Thanes stopped celebrating and turned to him with puzzled expressions where they usually wore their scowls.

'Nothing,' said the Dragon Lord. 'You say you have found the Star Stone?'

'Yes!' protested Fangar in a wounded voice.

'Well where is it?' said the Half-Dragon patiently.

Before Fangar could answer there was a moan from the back of the room. Balder had decided he didn't like being backed into a corner and he rumbled towards the door, swatting a couple of warriors like dragon flies.

Fangar looked up at the stars and down to the bear and howled in amazement.

'The Bear!' cried Fangar. 'He's come from the sky!'

This curious idea went around Fangar's war-pack like a plague of fleas. Even though they'd captured the goat and the bear when they seized Arnuf and me, the Dragons were in such a mead-muddled state that soon they were hailing Balder as a Star-bear and leading him off to meet their lord.

'Bring the goat too!' cried a Thane. Ragnar is among us! Thor's own goat has come down from the stars!'

The rest of the pack fell silent. They were waiting for the word of their Dragon-Lord, but instead they heard Hardlarder's grim voice.

'Stop this...' cried the dour Abbot. 'Stop it now! You... you, pack of heathens!'

'Yes we are,' said Fangar. 'And we're proud of it It's not every day you get such a close look at your gods. Imagine how happy you'd feel if your god came down through the roof for a visit?'

'Blasphemy!' cried the Abbot.

Fangar seized the monk by the throat. I hoped he'd

crack Hardlarder's nut but instead he dropped him.

'Take your heathen paws off me!' demanded the Brother. Slightly too late, if you ask me, because the Dragon raider had already thrown him to the ground.

'Save the Abbot!' howled Fastwagger.

'Remember your vow of silence Brother,' I said slipping a gag over his mouth.

Fangar ignored the muffled monk and turned to his master.

'This is a great day for you my Lord. We've found the Star Stone. And it has summoned the gods down from the stars. See! Two of them are here before us.'

The Half-Dragon was not convinced.

'Fangar,' he began, with menace gathering in his voice like a brewing storm. 'I see.... nothing.'

The old Dragon stormed out of the room with Fangar at his heels, followed by the rest of his pack, save for a couple of guards.

As my terror cooled to dread, I considered my plight. The was no escaping from the Dragons. I'd lied and saved my skin, but for how long?

'Why can't the Half-Dragon see the visions?' asked Fastwagger in a quivering voice.

'You might as well ask why Fangar *can* see them!' I growled.

Fangar burst back into the room.

'Well met my friend,' I began, but he'd been ordered not to take any more of my nonsense.

The next thing I felt was a crack on the brain-case, and everything went as dark as a night in Gnorway.

CHAPTER SEVENTEEN

SKALD HUNT

W hen I awoke, my head felt worse than a Berserker on the morning after his Brother's wedding. Everything thumped when I moved.

'Beowuff?' called Fastwagger. 'Beowuff? Are you alright.'

'I've felt better,' I moaned. 'The last time I felt this bad was when Arnuf put Helscaps in my water.'

Suddenly, I understood. Fangar and his war-pack had been at the monk-mead. The visions had been caused by the toadstool-laced brew. Only the Half-Dragon had refused to drink. No wonder he couldn't see the stars move. Fangar and his mates had drained the great mead kettle dry. They were so mead-muddled that if a crow flapped through the smoke-hole, I'd be able to convince them it was a shield-maiden belonging to Bodin the bearded Bonefather himself.

Fastwagger and I whispered to each other in the dark. We were still deciding what to do when three big Thanes came bursting in and dragged us back into the chronicle house in chains.

There was no sign of Fangar. I guess that he and his bench-mates were sleeping off their headaches. If I was right about the poisoned toadstools, they'd have woken up in even worse shape than old Beowuffer.

Through the gloom, I spotted a familiar figure –

deep in thought. He was scratching at a pile of stone slabs at the back of the room. They were intended for the roof of the chronicle house.

The Half-Dragon beckoned to me to approach and my heart began to hammer like a blacksmith on double-pay. When I was close enough to see the tattoo on his tongue, he leant in close and whispered.

'Which of these is the Star Stone?'

Before I could answer, Fastwagger spoke.

'If we tell you – do you promise to leave the Monastery of Sin Carne in peace and never return to our shores again?'

The Half-Dragon looked at the monk and nodded.

'Aye, I swear it!' he said.

I could not believe what I had just seen. The Brother had a crafty tongue on him. Not only had he just told a lie, he'd told it to the savage leader of a war-pack.

Fasterwagger pointed solemnly at one of the stones. I wished he'd chosen one that wasn't broken. He even dared to give me a knowing wink.

The Half-Dragon eyed the stone in wonder, a greedy smile spreading across his thin lips.

'My thanks,' he said softly.

Then he took a war-horn from his belt and blew a blast that crashed through my brain like an axe-blow.

As I was recovering my horn-blasted wits, Fangar and the rest of the pack trotted through the door, smirking like Swedes at a Gnorwegian burial.

'Seize the Stone!' commanded the Half-Dragon.

'Yes Lord,' barked Fanger, eager to do his master's axe-work.

'And then trample this miserable monk-hole into the dirt,' he added.

'What?' yelped Fasterwagger.

'You heard me! I want this place flatter then the whale-road!'

The young monk let out a horrified gasp.

'You lied!' said Fastwagger. 'Speaking falsely is an offense before...'

'Kill him! Kill them all!' raged the Half-Dragon.

We were witnessing his flaming rage. I was not surprised. You do not get to be the head of a Dragon clan by keeping your promises, or your temper.

Poor Fastwagger cast himself down and began to whimper, clutching at his cross-sticks.

'No!' he howled.

By chance, the Dragon-Lord had to pass by me as he left Fangar to do the dirty work.

I leaned in and managed to whisper in his ear.

'You can't do this,' I said.

'Why ever not?' laughed the Half-Dragon.

I have never been closer to Hel's gates than at this moment, when I interrupted him.

'Because of the Star Stone...,' I began.

An iron fist choked the rest of this sentence from me. Fangar drew his blade and raised it.

'... the stone gets its power...' I spluttered.

Fangar's master stayed his slaying paw.

'Wait!' ordered the Dragon Lord. 'Let's hear this. Go on, tell me before you die. Where does the Star Stone get its power from?'

'Monks,' I gasped.

'What?' laughed the Half-Dragon.

'Monks!' I cried, recovering my breath now that Fangar had loosened his death-grip.

'It takes monk-power to work the stone,' I repeated.

'Monks?' declared the Dragon Lord. 'Those muttering mumblers? I do not believe you!'

'It's the truth Lord. The stone used to be strong – until you started kidnapping monks and sailing off with them to.... Where is it that you sail them off to?'

'Dragongeld Island?' growled Fangar in amazement.

'Silence!!!' growled the Half-Dragon in a rage. He rounded on me, his jaws quivering. But I carried on speaking.

'Now there aren't enough monks to power the Star Stone,' I said. 'So it can't make the stars dance – do you see?'

In all my lying days, this untruth counts as one of my finest. The Dragon-Lord stood quietly for a moment, gazing at the stars through the unfinished roof. This lie was too grand, too impossible, too unbelievable. It was almost strange enough to be true.

Finally, Fangar spoke.

'I see what's needed! The stone wants monk-blood to get it working does it? Fine – say the word Lord and I'll have it running in streams.'

For some reason, Fangar had got it into his heathen skull that the stone wanted a sacrifice before it worked. Sacrificing to rocks or trees wasn't unusual. Bodin and the rest of the gods were a bloodthirsty pack.

Fangar charged off down the corridor on a monk-hunt and I had to whistle him back.

'No!' I cried. 'Monk-blood won't do it.'

'What then?' asked Fangar in a puzzled voice. 'Monk-bones? The Abbot's innards in a bucket?'

I put on my most pious face.

'The Star Stone needs...' I began, leaving a solemn pause. But my word-well had run dry and I did not know what to say.

'Songs,' said Fastwagger.

'Songs?' said the Half-Dragon, almost dropping his battle-axe in surprise.

'Er – yes!' I gasped, trying not to stare at Fastwagger in wonder and amazement. 'The young Brother here is right. And before you ask – howling won't do. The songs must be sung properly by expert chanters. You'll need monks, all moaning together to make the Star Stone work.'

'Bring all the monks here,' commanded the Half-Dragon. 'Round them up!'

The Dragon-pack soon had every monk in Sin Carne crammed into the chronicle house and chanting. Fangar and his Lord gazed through the hole in the roof, waiting for the stars to start dancing.

But nothing happened. Fangar seemed even more

disappointed than we were.

The toadstool-laced mead must have worn off, and although he squinted and gazed and turned his head, he saw nothing but pale stars and some wisps of cloud-murk in the winter sky. And that was all that he was going to see, unless I found a way to get more monk-mead down his sup-hole.

'All of this singing is thirsty work,' I began. 'Shall I call for some mead to...'

'Silence!' cried Fangar. 'Why isn't it working?'

I racked my brain, but it was no use. The lake of lies within my brain-case had dried up again. I could not think of an answer. Fangar ran his claws down the blade of his axe. I thought I was lost, but Fastwagger spoke once more.

'We need more monks,' he said sadly. 'Isn't that right Brother Beowuff?'

'More monks you say?' said Fangar. 'Where in Bodin's name are we going to find more of the beggars?'

I racked my brain trying to think, lost in a whirlpool of my own nonsense. Then I heard myself saying something strange.

'A word please,' I whispered. 'Lord, send your pack away – for you might find what I am about to tell you a little bit distasteful.'

'My Thanes have strong bellies,' said the Half-Dragon.

'No doubt Lord – but what I am about to tell you would turn the stomach of any honourable war-dog.'

The Dragon Lord raised his nose and sniffed.

Then he told Fangar to leave us alone.

'Is this wise Lord?' growled the Dragon's Thanes.

'These monks are weak-toothed whelps,' laughed their leader. 'I could snap this one's back with a paw-swipe. And the other is a monk. I doubt that you will have to avenge my death.'

'As you wish Lord,' said Fangar.

When the chamber was empty save for Fastwagger and me, the Dragon Lord grew impatient.

'Now weak-paws, what is it that you would tell me in secret? Quick – before I tear your tongues out!'

'The Star Stone is powered by songs...' I began.

'Yes...' he interrupted impatiently.

'The songs need to be chanted by monks...'

'Yes! So you have said – go on...'

'Well Lord – what I have said is not strictly true. The Stone will work as long as the songs are sung by those who have given up...'

My voice trailed off and silence ruled the hall.

'What?' ordered the Dragon-Lord. 'Tell me,'

'Meat,' I muttered.

'Urrrgh!' spat the Half-Dragon, clutching his belly.

'The songs must be sung by dogs who have eaten no flesh for a month – or their prayers will be unworthy.'

'What?' boomed the Dragon-Lord.

Fastwagger looked at me in wonder, and then nodded.

'Give up meat for a month?' he muttered. 'No dog of

honour could stand it.'

'Aye Lord. But if your pack would join in the fast – we could turn them into monk-singers.'

'Meatless Dragons? raged the sea-king. 'Word would spread to all the other war-packs. We'd be the joke of the Whale road. They'd be yapping about it from here to the bay of the Vik. Isn't there another way?'

I shook my head. Fastwagger followed my lead.

'Sorry Lord,' I said.

I was wondering whether he'd order Fangar to have me flailed or crushed when a clear voice broke the silence.

'We could fetch the Skald,' said Fastwagger.

Although I had forgotten my weak-witted bench-mate Arnuf, who was back on the Dragon-boat, it seemed that Fastwagger had remembered him.

The Half-Dragon eyed him in the way that a wildcat eyes a baby sparrow that has fallen from the nest.

'So it's Skalds that we need now is it?' growled the Half-Dragon. 'You just said that meatless monks must do the singing.'

'The Skald is fasting,' said Fastwagger. 'He has also sworn to forsake flesh for a month...'

The Half-Dragon was as cunning as a snake, but he was also greedy. He wanted that Star Stone more than anything else in the three-ringed disc of this world.

A few moments later, he was whistling Fangar back into the room.

'Fetch the other Skald immediately!' he commanded.

'The one who was half-trained.'

Fangar let out a frightened whimper.

'I cannot fetch him Lord...' he moaned.

'Why not?' growled the Dragon.

'He's already headed for the Hagsmouth,' answered Fangar. 'He tried to stop us shooting seagulls...'

'Find him!' ordered the Half-Dragon. 'Or you and your crew will taste no meat for a month.'

When they heard the Dragon-Lord's order to rescue Arnuf from the whirlpool, every dog in the place bolted for his long boat, save for a small huddle of Thanes who were left behind to guard the Star Stone.

Unfortunately, Fangar insisted that I went with him.

'To the Hagsmouth!' he cried as his war-pack clambered aboard their fastest ship.

The tide was on the turn and an east wind filled the sails. Luckily for Arnuf, Fangar's longboat was a swift vessel. A true sea-cutter, with a thin prow that sliced through the waves with the force of a spear-point. Unluckily for Arnuf, The Hagsmouth was the most feared whirlpool in the North. Every sailor knew of it. In ancient days, the islanders used to float prisoners out there to be swallowed by the whirling sea. But the sport-spoiling monks of Sin Carne had put a stop to that tradition. Curse their rotten cowls.

As we neared the straggling rocks, Fangar growled his orders.

'Not too close Helmspaw! You'll wreck us!'

The sea was choppy and tongues of foam licked at

the black stones. There wasn't any sign of the whirlpool save for some bumpy water. The Hag lurked in secret until you were right inside her craggy jaws. Once she'd sucked you in, there was no way out.

'It's useless,' moaned Fangar. 'That Skald is Hag's bait already.'

We were about to turn back to shore when the look-out began to yap excitedly.

'Over there!' he cried.

Clinging to a weed-clad rock was a dark shape. It looked for all the world like a sea-swamped sack of rubbish that had been slung off a longboat. Then I spotted a familiar snout sticking out, bobbing up and down like a loot-picker on a battlefield.

'Don't sit there cringing like mound-sniffers!' barked Fangar. 'Grab a line someone! Swim out and get him.'

My cowardly blood ran cold. I skulked in a lowly manner, praying to all the gods I could think of that Fangar wasn't expecting me to rescue Arnuf.

At last, one of the Thanes sprang up and followed Fangar's order. He was a fat, wolf-jawed hound with hair as stiff as hedgehog spines.

Cheers and jeers rang out around the boat as Jawkeld dived off the side and struck out towards Arnuf's rock.

'That's the last we'll see of him,' said a low voice.

'I wager he'll never make it,' said a brindled hound.

'I'll take that bet,' cried one of the Thanes. 'Jawkeld swims like a great white shark.'

'Like a great fat shark, you mean,' said his mate.

The boat boomed with their jeers as Jawkeld closed in on Arnuf. The mastiff was right. I've never seen a dog swim so fast.

'Go on Jawkeld!' cried the dogs who'd bet on him.

He shot towards Arnuf like an eel up a sewer-pipe.

The crew fell silent as the sea-dog shot straight past Arnuf and disappeared into the dark water.

'The current's got him,' said the brindled hound. 'They don't call it the Hagsmouth for nothing She's swallowed him down. I'll have my money now.'

'Come on sea-slugs,' called Fangar. 'Who's next?'

Some of the dogs laughed and others muttered, then the boat fell quiet.

It takes a lot to silence a pack of war-dogs, but Fangar had just managed it.

'Are you in jest Fangar?' asked a black mastiff.

'Do I ever jest?' answered Fangar. 'The Half-Dragon wants that Skald rescuing. He's ordered me to get it done. Which of you whelps wants to tell him we've disobeyed his orders?'

There was silence.

'I thought not,' growled Fangar. 'So who's next?'

Have you guessed who they chose? I'll spare the details about how I begged and grovelled and ran about the ship and then pleaded and so on, for you all know old Beowuffer too well by now. You can be sure I tried every trick to wriggle out of it. But they all failed.

I was hag-bait for sure. But at least I had the good sense to get them to tie a line around my middle first.

'Take hold of the rope lads,' cried Fangar. 'Once Beowuff has the Skald, I'll give the command and we'll haul 'em both back.'

'Wait,' I howled, 'tie it tighter than that...'

But as these words were leaving my lips, I was already leaving the longboat. Fangar had given me a push of encouragement.

The sea was colder than a widow's hut. I didn't do much swimming, because the current had me in its grip. Soon I was shooting toward's Arnuf's rock like a stone from a slingshot.

'Strike out for the left!' called a voice from behind.

Spewing out sea-water, I got my nose up and saw a terrible sight. That fabled line of straggling rocks, the fang-like reef that had claimed hundreds of ships.

I was nearly at Arnuf's float-sack, close enough to see where it had been tangled. But the current was dragging me straight towards the Hagsmouth.

In a fury, I flailed at the cruel waves, trying to drag myself towards Arnuf. If I could get a hold of the float sack, then Fangar's crew could haul me back. But I was sinking, pulled under the waves as if by invisible paws.

'Noooooooo!!!' I spluttered, choking like a whale with a blocked blow-hole.

'Beowuff?' cried my half drowned bench-mate. 'Beowuff is that you?'

Then I heard the screeching cry of a seagull and felt a beak spearing at my backside.

'Aaaarggh!' I wailed, in anticipation of the pain.

'It is you!' called Arnuf. 'Thank you bench-mate.'

'Get off me!' I cried, trying to get a paw out of the water to flail at the winged menace that was coming at me from above. I felt its wings on my snout and its beak on my back.

'Get off me you flapping devil!' I cried. 'Shoo! You white-feathered menace!'

The gull, as you may have guessed, had not been trying to beak me to death, as I thought at the time. She had got a hold of the rope around my waist, so as to try to steer me towards Arnuf.

'Valki! Valki!' cried Arnuf reaching for my paw. 'You've saved us! What a good gull!'

Urged on by Fangar's bone-whip, the crew pulled on the rope like oxen at the plough. Alas, it was a long haul back to the boat. By the time they'd towed us in and cut Arnuf out of the bull-skin bag, I was shaking with cold. Arnuf was frothing and babbling like a dammed-brook and spewing up sea-water by the bucket load. The war-dogs found this highly amusing, but Fangar was not known for his sense of humour.

'He's spouting like a whalefish!' laughed the Helms-paw. 'Perhaps he'll drown right here on deck?'

'Shut it!' growled Fangar. 'If he croaks, you'll be the next to kiss the Hagsmouth.'

The helmspaw didn't like sound of this and went back to his place muttering a string of curses that would have made a war-troll drop his club.

At last Arnuf struggled to his feet.

'He lives!' cheered a dog. 'I'll have my money now.'

'Can we get you anything Brother?' asked Fangar, in an unusually kind voice. Then he let out a bark and the cook came forward with a tray of deer-steaks and a cup of hot meat-mead. My gut sack went all squelchy at the sight of these flesh-treats.

Fangar laughed a wicked laugh and I realised that this was a trial. They planned to see if my story about Arnuf's meat-free diet was true. This had the scent of the The Half-Dragon about it. He was a cunning old ogre if ever there was one.

Fangar smiled a yellow smile as the meat-mead was offered.

'Arnuf! Brother Arnuf? Can you hear me?' I began.

But Fangar clamped his paw over my mouth.

Arnuf took the drinking horn in a shaking paw and supped long and hard.

Fangar pulled his gutting knife out of its sheath. I thought that all was lost. I was about to be slit like a haddock and cast down the Hagsmouth.

But as soon the meat-mead hit Arnuf's stomach, it bounced back up and drenched the deck like the death-spout of a wounded whale.

'Urrrrrgh!' he moaned.

'You see?' I called triumphantly. His gut-sack has rejected the meat-mead, just as I said it would. He make a perfect prayer-singer.'

Fangar grunted and slid the knife back into its leather sheath. He wouldn't be filleting us just yet.

'Set course for the monastery,' he ordered.

Chapter Eighteen

The Hermit

When we reached Sin Carne, they marched us straight to the chronicle house. There was no sign of the Half-Dragon, but the monks were praying up a storm.

'Arnuf,' I began to warn in a whisper, 'listen...'

But Fangar soon stopped me with a stern growl.

'Sing!' he roared. 'Pray harder, you woeful whelps!'

He raised his bone-whip high in the air and cracked it against the stone pews, by way of encouragement.

The monks raised their voices to the skies and began to moan and clamour. No matter how hard they chanted, nothing happened. Without more Helscaps to lace the monk-mead with, the stars weren't going to do any more dancing.

Suddenly the door gaped open and in came a pair of Dragon warriors, dragging a string of unfortunate captives behind them.

At the end of the line was Billi, our goat, on a long rope. The chronicle house was now packed tighter than a Swedlander's sausage.

Abbot Hardlarder, who was sat next to Fastwagger, leapt up and shook his shackles.

'Brother Goodoldboyson?' he called. 'Don't say they've got you as well. They are forcing us to take part in this heathen ceremony...'

The ancient monk clasped his paws together.

'Billi!' I called. 'You know about herb-lore. Where can we get some more Helscaps? We must find them – or we are dead meat.'

'I'm jiggered if I ken,' replied the goat. 'I'm a hundred miles from hame.'

No one else had any ideas.

'Think Brothers!' I cried. 'Your lives depend on it.'

At last a voice spoke up from the back. 'The hermit of Farne is wise in herb-lore...' called one of the monks.

'Thank Thor for that,' cried Arnuf.

'Forgive him Brothers,' I said. 'He knows not what he is on about.'

Goodoldboyson nodded. Hardlarder scowled at Arnuf and gripped his cross-sticks.

'Where does this hermit dwell?' I asked.

'On the Farne islands,' said Fastwagger. 'He guards the Bones of St Cuthbert.'

'This Cuthbert?', I began with my gut-sack rumbling. 'He's got a decent bone-hoard has he?'

'You misunderstand me,' said Fastwagger. 'It is St Cuthbert's own bones that are in the cave. The Hermit guards his resting place.'

'I see. And he'd give us his Helscaps would he?'

'Silence!' said Hardlarder. 'Don't speak heathen names in this place.'

'Sorry,' I spluttered. 'I mean, he'd give us some more toadstools would he?'

'I doubt it,' said Hardlarder.

'It is a lonely life on the island and he has spent a

long time alone with his thoughts...' began Fastwagger.

'He wakes up sane,' said Hardlarder. 'But by noon he's the maddest monk from here to the Iceland shore.'

'It might work,' said Fastwagger. 'Beowuff, will you go to Farne and find the toadstools?'

Fastwagger was clearly trying for second place on the list of crazed clerics.

'So you would have me row to a sea-wracked rock and fetch Helscaps from a half-crazed hermit who guards a grave in a cave?' I muttered.

'I know that I ask a lot...' began Fastwagger.

'You do indeed,' I growled. 'Why not go yourself?'

'My place is here, with my Brothers,' he replied.

'I see,' I said flatly.

The Brothers were as battle-shy as old Beowuff. They always had an excuse to keep themselves safe.

'I hope you monks can work wonders,' I said. 'If I'm supposed to walk out of here, get past Fangar and his pack and swim to the Farne Islands and back.'

Fastwagger shook his head solemnly.

'Brother Harfruff has a boat, hidden in the sand dunes, which is well stocked with fodder,' he explained.

I could hardly believe my ears. A boat full of monk-biscuits? I willed my tail not to wag for fear that it would give me away.

'We have thought about how to get past Fangar's pack,' began Fastwagger. 'Tonight, you and your brave friend...'

'All right! All right! I'll go,' I sighed.

CHAPTER NINETEEN

SHIP OF FOOLS

Fastwagger had done some cunning plotting, for a cleric. The prayer-sayer had managed to convince Fangar that the monks needed mead and asked whether his pack fancied a refreshing brew as well. Does night follow day? Of course Fangar agreed and naturally he had to allow Fastwagger out of the chronicle house to fire up his mead-kettle. Arnuf and I exchanged clothes with two of the Brothers and followed Fastwagger down the corridors. Before we knew it, we'd made it as far as the brewing hall.

'May He watch over you on your mission,' called Fastwagger. Then he turned and trotted slowly back towards the his mead-kettle. As we left, the chants of the unfortunate monks echoed down the corridor.

Outside, the night was warm and a harvest moon was rising in the North.

'It's a fine night for a walk,' said Arnuf. 'It was kind of Fangar to let us help with the mead brewing. And it was good of Fastwagger to offer to pray for us.'

'Listen Arnuf,' I said. 'I beg you, be silent when we reach the gates. Let no words pass your lips or we will be slain on the spot.'

When we reached the gates, we were to tell the guards that we were brewers, off to draw water.

'Halt!' commanded the gate-guard. 'By whose orders

164

do you walk freely about?'

'By Lord Fangar's orders,' I replied. 'He has sent us to fetch water for the next brew of mead.'

'Draw your water from the well, you weak-wits,' growled the lurcher at the gate.

'We can't,' I explained. 'The well has been poisoned.'

'Shut it monk!' ordered the lurcher. 'Before I tear you a second prayer-hole.'

'As you wish,' I answered. 'Tis' a pity there'll be no mead to sup tonight.'

Furious growls came from the watch tower, and before I'd taken ten steps down the path, he called me back.

'You need fresh water to brew your monk-mead, you say?' called the lurcher, licking his lips.

'Aye,' said Arnuf, forgetting my order that he keep his mouth shut.

'Go on then,' he called. 'Go about your business.'

Arnuf started to cock his leg.

'Not that sort of business!' I growled, striking him on the nose.

The great oak gate began to open.

'Thank you gate-guard,' I replied.

'Be warned!' growled the guard. 'I've my eye on you Go to the river and come straight back. Understood?'

'Understood. We monks have sworn not to tell lies,' I added. 'It is against our sacred law.'

'You may pass!' called the guard.

'Not that sort of pass!' I growled, seeing that Arnuf was swinging his leg up to the gatepost for the second time. 'Stop it Arnuf! No more leaking.'

The gate swung wide open and we slipped out into the warm evening.

'Bless you,' I called to the guard, thinking myself clever to have remembered to speak like a monk.

'May Thor protect you!' added Arnuf.

If weak-wits had their own kingdom, Arnuf would be crowned prince!

'May Thor protect you?' I growled. 'Fastwagger's lot worship the cross-god, not Thor and his war-pack!'

'Sorry Beowuff!' he whimpered.

'Shut your snout and keep walking,' I cursed. 'And pray that the gate-guard is as big a fool as you are.'

Step followed step, paw followed paw, breath followed breath as we edged towards the causeway with the harvest moon throwing its light on our backs. The water was at its lowest point and the step-stones stood out like a rope of grey pearls against the black water.

As I set my paw onto the first stone, I thought I had made it. Then I heard shouts from the gate.

My heart leapt up from my gut-sack into my maw.

'What do we do?' asked Arnuf in a panic.

'Keep walking!' I cried. 'And don't stop till you're across the water.'

'Brothers?' growled the gate-guard. 'Brothers! Come back! I have a question to ask...'

But the guard was cut off in mid sentence. There was

no cry, only a hard thud as the guard fell dead to the ground.

'It's must be a miracle!' cried Arnuf, clutching at his cross-sticks. He was right.

Only when we were across the water did I dare to look back towards Sin Carne. I hoped it was the last time I'd ever see that miserable monk-hole.

Brother Harfruff's boat was easy to find. That fool of a monk cannot have done much 'boat hiding' before. It had been dragged half way out of the bushes and its prow was in plain sight of the beach. True to his word, the monk had stocked it full of all manner of provisions. None of them contained meat. But there was fresh water in skins, and monk-biscuits and dried fruits a plenty.

As I struggled to haul the boat out, Arnuf raised his nose to the stars and stared silently.

'Don't stand there gaping like Gorm the Gormless,' I growled. 'Lend a paw.'

'Beowuff,' he began in a worried tone.

'What?' I answered.

'How will we know where the Farne Islands are?'

Arnuf was worried about how to find the Farne Islands. I'd rather seek for a bogey in a Swedelander's snot-rag! However, I did not tell him that.

'Help me with the boat,' I sighed. 'We'll worry about that later.'

'Look at the sand,' he cried in wonder.

I saw that a large arrow had been drawn in the sands pointing to the west. Two crossed sticks like the ones that the monks wear had been placed above the arrow.

'I have a feeling that the arrow is pointing to Farne,' said Arnuf. 'I think we should follow it.'

I carried on dragging the boat towards the waves.

Arnuf leapt aboard and took his place at the oars.

The first half mile was hard rowing on account of the strong current.

'Put your back into it Arnuf,' I cried, stuffing as many monk biscuits into my mouth as I could.

'When will it be your turn to row?' moaned my weak-witted companion.

'When that mangy monk-hole and the Dragon ships are all out of sight,' I explained. 'Keep rowing! You're doing a good job.'

At last, when Arnuf was panting hard from his oar work, I agreed to let him rest.

'Thank you Beowuff,' he said solemnly.

'Don't thank me too soon,' I replied. 'You'll be starting again in a moment.'

'No,' he said seriously. 'I mean, thank you for helping the monks. It is no small thing you are doing.'

When I did not answer, he held me with his gaze.

'Beowuff?' he growled accusingly.

'Did I say I'd help the monks? I growled.

'Beowuff!' he gasped in horror.

'"I'll go," is what I said, and I am going, aren't I? Only I'm not going to come back. You can return and die with your monk-Brothers, if you are so minded. I'm sure that Fangar and his crew can find room for one more body in their slain-pile.'

Arnuf didn't answer. He just looked at me with that nobler-than-you expression and put down the oars.

'Keep rowing Arnuf!' I demanded.

But he shook his head. Not a word left his lips.

'Please!' I said nicely, offering him a biscuit from the bag, which I had placed at my end of the boat.

He gave another silent shake of the head.

'Arnuf, if you don't row, you don't eat,' I warned.

He ignored me, turning his nose back in the direction of Sin Carne.

'Fine!' I growled, snatching the oars. 'I'll do it myself.'

Well bench-mates, old Beowuffer is not a strong rower, unlike some dogs who can labour all day at the oars. I soon tired of the task. I had meant to travel down the coast and away from the monastery and the teeth of the dragon-pack. But the tide and the winds were taking me out to sea.

The moon was still high in the sky when I realised what was happening.

'Arnuf!' I begged. 'Take a turn at the oars, or we'll be lost.'

Again that clam-mouthed fool simply shook his head and tutted at me.

High in the sky, a lonely gull let out a mournful cry.

Exhausted, I cast the oars into the bottom of the boat and let sleep roll over me.

CHAPTER TWENTY

LAST ORDERS

When I awoke, I found that the wind had died and the sea was as flat as a monk-biscuit. The boat hardly rocked at all but the birds were singing. Raising my nose from the sea-swamped boards, I rubbed my eyes.

One of the fattest pigeons I have ever seen landed on the prow and lunged at my biscuit sack.

'Get away! You feathered food-snatcher!' I cried, kicking at its beak and missing. To my horror, I felt the boat rocking wildly. I tumbled out and splashed around in terror in the icy water.

'Help! Help! Arnuf!' I cried. 'I'm drowning!'

My desperate eyes fixed on the boat, but there was no sign of Arnuf. My paws scrambled about in panic, as a wave broke over my snout and sucked me below.

'Arnuf!' I cried, spitting out seaweed. 'Save me! Before I drown!'

'Do you swear to return to help the monks?' called a familiar voice.

'Aye!' I spluttered. 'I swear on my mother Mingingfrith's death-mound!'

'Alright,' said Arnuf. 'Hang on.'

With an enormous splash, he threw himself into the water beside me and began to flail his legs around madly. Great arcs of foaming water flew through the air.

'What are you doing!!!!' I raged.

'Joining you,' said Arnuf.

He stopped thrashing around in the water for a moment. 'Nice morning for a swim,' he added, standing up.

I am not at my best in the morning. The water we stood in was shallow, although the waves were rolling in and breaking on the sandy beach.

Once again, I found that I'd been washed up on a strange shore. Birds flocked in the trees, rabbits ran in the heather. I expect that fat fish probably swarmed like bees in the shallows, for that matter.

'Come over here,' he said. 'I want to show you something.'

Knowing Arnuf, it was probably a nest made of seaweed, or an unusual line of whelks in a row. For such things hold more wonder for him than bone-hoards and treasure-piles do for the rest of us.

'It's a bag,' announced Arnuf proudly. 'And you'll never guess what is inside it.'

'Nothing,' I guessed.

'Wrong,' he laughed.

'Seawater?' I offered.

'Wrong again,' he replied.

'Treasure?' I gasped.

'Beowuff,' he said. 'It's stranger than you'll ever guess.'

'Arnuf,' I began. 'Although we may have days, weeks or even years of fun together on this deserted island. I'm already growing tired of your 'what's in the sack?' game. Why don't you run off and chase some seagulls?'

'Look!' said Arnuf, throwing the bag over to me.

It was made of tough leather, and tied at the neck with strong cord. I undid the knot and looked inside.

'Helscaps!' I gasped. 'Where did you find them?'

'Here,' said Arnuf. 'Right here on the beach.'

Lost for words, I stared at the bag and gasped.

'That's not all,' said Arnuf. 'I found three waterskins and a bag of biscuits as well. This cannot have happened by chance. It is as if we are being... helped!'

Clutching his cross-sticks, he gazed to the heavens.

I kept my nose at ground-level and sniffed around for a sign.

It was not long before I'd spotted it. High on the hillside was the gaping mouth of a dark cave.

'The Hermit,' I gasped, grabbing the food sack and running back down the beach.

'Where are we going now?' called Arnuf. 'Are we going to greet the Hermit?'

'By noon, The Hermit of Farne is the maddest monk in the North,' I pointed out. 'I expect that he won't be best pleased to find his food gone and his herb-bag robbed.'

I rolled my eyes and muttered under my breath.

'Arnuf,' I said as we climbed back into the boat. 'Answer me true. Did you go up to that cave and steal the Helscaps and the food from the Hermit?'

'I didn't rob anyone,' he answered indignantly.

'Beowuff, I tell you we are being helped, by an invisible paw, just like Fastwagger said...'

'Silence!' I cried. 'Get rowing, unless you want your bones to lie next to St Cuthbert's in that hermit hole.'

Well bench-mates, although the island had fresh water and food a plenty, I was glad to be back in my open boat with the wind raging. The idea of a mad monk bent on revenge had soured the idea of a stay on the Farne Islands. Where should old Beowuff point the prow of his sea-cutter? I had no clue where I was, and rather than 'striking out across the boundless seas,' like they do in the sagas, I thought it would be best to sneak back to the coast under the cover of darkness.

My kitten-witted companion laboured long at the oars and for a while, all went well.

I steered a little to the east of our original course, for on no account did I want to wind up in that unlucky monk-hole again. My mother Mingingfrith does not have a death-mound, in case you were wondering about the vow I swore earlier.

When sleep finally took me, I raced though the whole night in an eye-blink and woke to the sound of Arnuf, calling like a hoot-owl.

'Helloooooo! Hellooooo!' he howled, leaping up and down and almost overturning out boat. 'I think they've seen us,' he said brightly.

'What? Who's seen us?' I said warily. Then I fell back down to continue my slumbers. Knowing Arnuf, he'd probably made friends with some passing jellyfish.

'They're over there,' he said.

Grumbling, I hauled myself up to have a look. In the distance I could clearly make out the shadow of a ship.

'Arnuf!' I moaned. 'What are you doing?'

'Waving,' he replied, 'At that longboat.'

By now, the mystery sea-cutter had changed tack and was headed straight towards us.

'Arnuf!' I screamed. 'Does anything about that ship look familiar?'

He scratched his head and sat with a weak-witted grin spreading across his snout.

'See that ugly great monster on the prow?' I continued. 'Does that remind you of anything?'

He peered into the gloom and squinted.

'Looks like a dragon to me,' he replied.

'Who do we know who sails in a Dragon-ship?'

'Don't tell me. I'll get it,' he said, scratching his ear.

'I'll give you a clue,' I said. 'It's a war-pack who tied you up in a bull-skin bag and threw you down the Hagspout.'

'Fangar?' he cried.

In the beat of a gull's wing, his expression of triumph turned to dread, and then to terror.

'You lump-brained loon! You're waving at the Dragon raiders!'

Like a pair of fattened pigeons on a seed-sack, we'd been sitting merrily, without expecting the hawk to strike.

Fangar had sent his war-pack off to search for us, by

order of the Half-Dragon.

Soon we were taken and bound and headed for Sine Carne once again. It was to be a grim homecoming. For some reason, the Half-Dragon wanted us alive and whole. It was lucky for us that he'd given clear orders, for I am sure that many on that boat were skilled in the art of throat-ripping. Fangar himself was not on board, so it was one of his trusted Thanes, a lurcher, that was yanking my chain as he marched me down the causeway. I remember thinking that I had already trod this lonely road far too many times. Surely my good fortune was set to run out.

A mastiff with paws the size of oar-blades hauled at Arnuf's collar.

'Move!' growled the lurcher, twisting my chain.

I sighed and gazed out across the slate-grey waves. The whale-road lapped against the stones and the wind blew freezing foam into my face. The water looked even more inviting than it had done before. I dreaded to think what terrors the Half-Dragon had dreamed up for me. You don't get to be the leader of a war-pack without having the very worst kind of imagination.

I was wondering whether to slip into the waves when I heard a muffled shout and then a splash. When I swung myself around in a panic, there was no sign of the either the lurcher or the mastiff.

'Thor's bolts!' I gasped. 'What happened to Fangar's Thanes?'

Arnuf rubbed at the cross-sticks around his collar.

'I told you Beowuff,' he said seriously. 'Someone is watching over us, just like Fastwagger promised.'

A squawk tore through the air and I heard the beat of wings above me.

'You don't mean that stinky old seagull do you?' I asked suspiciously. 'She can flap-off for all I care.'

'I'm not talking about Valki...' said Arnuf, thrusting a paw into his pocket. 'You know who I mean. The miracle-maker that the monks talk about.'

Now normally I do not place any faith in charms and spells, but good fortune seemed to be following our footsteps. I thought about our lucky escape from Sine Carne; finding the Farne Islands so easily, the food that had been left on the beach and finding the Helscaps...

I gazed up to the sky and wondered. Were we puppets, dancing to the pull of an unseen paw?

Arnuf was convinced. When we reached the gates, he stood gawping, as if waiting for them to swing open by themselves. I gave them a hard shove and they creaked open on their hinges, revealing the familiar courtyard.

'That's weird,' I said. 'Where are the Dragons?'

Arnuf had an explanation, but I ignored him as we made our way inside the monastery.

As we passed the great mead-kettle, vapours were rising from its spout.

'Fastwagger!' cried Arnuf, spotting a shape at the top of the ladder.

'Skaldi!' cried the monk, almost toppling off the ladder. 'And Brother Beowuff! You've been delivered!'

'Aye!' said Arnuf. 'It was just as you said, we were protected all the way.'

'Thank goodness!' said Fastwagger. 'Do you have what we seek?'

'The Helscaps?' I asked.

Fastwagger grew silent at the mention of the toadstools, as if I had just leaked all over his family's rune-stone. I threw him the leather pouch and he added the dreaded caps to the mixture. A sweet gamey smell filled the room and the mead in the kettle began to bubble.

'Not all of them!' I cried.

The fool of a monk had put enough Helscaps in there to poison an army.

'Beowufffffffffff!' snarled a familiar voice from the bottom of the ladder. I did not need to look down.

It was my old friend Fangar, with his hench-mates in tow.

'Got you!' snarled the Half-Dragon's helper.

'What dirty work have you been doing Beowuff?' he asked, sniffing the air. 'Back-stabbing, I'll be bound.'

'Fear not,' whispered Arnuf, turning to Fastwagger. 'Watch this!'

Arnuf clutched his cross-sticks and began to mutter.

I was half expecting Fangar's pack to drop dead. But nothing happened.

'Beowuff?' roared Fangar. 'Beowuff! Answer me you bolt-battle.'

'I will speak to the Half-Dragon alone,' I called.

My words were brave but the quaking of my war-shy limbs had set the ladder trembling like a stranded Swede on a Danish beach.

'Give me your message while you still have a tongue to tell it,' demanded an ancient and wicked voice.

It was the Half-Dragon himself.

I lost my footing and slipped down a couple of rungs, willing my lying tongue to get to work.

'We have been on a pilgrimage Half-Dragon,' I called, falsehood dripping from my tongue like honey from a mead spoon.

'A pilgrimage?' repeated the wicked one.

'He means a sacred journey,' explained Arnuf.

'I know what a pilgrimage is, you cur!' snarled the Half-Dragon. 'I eat pilgrims for breakfast!'

'Pay no heed Lord,' I said, clouting Arnuf around the muzzle. 'He comes from a family of blacksmiths. They used to use his head for an anvil.'

'An anvil?' hissed the Half-Dragon. 'We'll do the same with yours. First, where have you been?'

'We travelled to the Holy Island of Farne,' I replied in a shaking voice. 'And now that Arnuf and I are purified – your Star Stone is sure to work.'

With a wild laugh, I ripped the bung from Brewboiler and a stream of monk-mead flowed out of the kettle.

'Drink! Drink! One and all!' I called heartily. 'This meatless mead will set the Star-Stone working!'

It does not take much to convince a pack of war-dogs to get after the mead.

Fangar's Thanes fell howling, thrusting their noses into the drink-spout until they had almost drained the great kettle dry.

'You too Lord,' I said quietly, taking my life in my paws as I offered him the mead. 'It is an important part of the ceremony.'

'This had better work,' said the Half-Dragon, taking a long slug from the drinking horn. 'Bring them to the chronicle house.'

As we entered the dark chamber, the unfortunate monk-pack were still chained to their pews.

I noticed that a green log from a young oak had been placed at the far end of the room. Next to this sprouting branch was a length of rope. Beside it, I spied a long knife with a nick in the blade. Tied to this forest alter, was our young friend Billi. It looked as if Fangar still had his own ideas about how to set the Stone to work.

'Beowuff!' bleated Billi. 'I dinnae like this. I've heard terrible tales of places like this.'

'Have no fear,' said Goodoldboyson. 'We are a peaceful order. We've sworn to harm no living thing.'

'It's not you monks I'm afeared of,' said Billi.

'Filthy heathens!' cried Hardlarder. 'I'll not let them stain this place with their sacrifices.'

'I'm glad tae hear it!' said Billi. 'But I'm nae sure ye or any of yer pack can stop them.'

Fangar picked up his knife and licked the blade, then he stumbled over a pew and began to threaten some monks. He'd obviously mislaid his bone-whip.

'Ye'd better get yon Star Stone working Beowuff!' bleated Billi. 'And be quick aboot it!'

I paid no heed to this, for I could not take my eyes off the Half-Dragon. The old monster had not uttered a word since he'd swigged our poisoned mead. The Dragon-Lord was a willing sinner, but I doubt that mead guzzling was one of his regular crimes. Now he stood reeling, as his cold heart pumped the toadstool-laced mead around his withered frame. His eyes began to roll and his black tongue lolled out of the side of his mouth like a rag worm from its sand-hole.

'The Stone!' he moaned. 'Bring me the Stone.'

Unfortunately he was talking to me.

I rushed over to the alter where a number of stones had been placed. Then I let out a string of chants which are seldom heard in a monastery.

'Arnuf!' I cried. 'Arnuf you gnat-witted pit-sniffer! Get over here now.'

He trotted over grinning like a seagull that had found two fish heads, and didn't know which one to peck first.

'What?' he laughed.

I feared that he too had been at the monk-mead.

'Which of these is the Star Stone?' I muttered. 'I have forgotten which one we said was sacred.'

'Bring forth the stone!' commanded the Dragon-Lord in a grim voice.

'Sorry Lord,' I replied. 'The Stone is a bit heavy for me to, er... bring forth on my own.'

'Bring the Stone!' hissed the old creature again. 'And Fangar! Make these prayer-sayers chant louder! I can hardly hear them!'

'Pray louder!' commanded Fangar. A sizzling crack told me that he'd managed to find his bone-whip.

'It's that big brown one, I think,' said Arnuf, pointing at a large slab.

'I want to see the stars dance!' said the Half-Dragon in a death-rage. 'Fangar! You promised!'

'I'm surprised they're not dancing already Lord.'

This much was true, considering the amount of toadstool-laced brew he'd just quaffed.

As I struggled to get a grip on the stone, Fastwagger approached.

'Why isn't it working?' he whispered. 'Why can't he see anything?'

I did not have the answer. There were enough Helscaps in that last batch of mead to stun a stone-giant. Perhaps old scale-face wasn't the vision-seeing type?

Frustrated at the delay, the Half-Dragon called Fangar to his side.

I could not hear what was said, but Fangar howled in triumph.

'Let's try the Old Ways. We'll see if Bodin and Thor can give the monk-magic a helping paw.'

'Forgive him,' called Brother Goodoldboyson, from a nearby pew. 'He knows not what he says.'

'It's nae what he says that I'm afeared of,' bleated Billi, tugging at his leash. He could not break free, he was tied to the alter.

'The Old Ways!' slurred the Half-Dragon, who had slumped down upon the alter. A cruel grin spread over his face and he threw the goat's leash to Fangar.

'Do it!' cried the Dragon-Lord. 'Bodin and his pack are thirsty.'

Fangar laughed and sprang towards Billi.

Luckily, the feckless Thane had taken on so much mead that he was swaying like a ship at anchor and the goat dodged out of his grasp.

'No Fangar!' barked Arnuf.

But Fangar had seized the goat's leash and was already raising his blade.

'You'll pay for this heathens!' cried Hardlarder. 'You'll not stain this sacred house with goat-blood.'

'Stop it Fangar!' cried Arnuf.

'Why?' laughed Fangar, waving his knife in my bench-mate's face.

'Because... killing is wrong,' whimpered Arnuf.

But Fangar had already stopped. He fell instantly to the floor, still clutching his long knife in his paw.

The Dragon pack let out a terrible howl. Slaver and drool dripping from their filed teeth, they sprang forward to avenge their captain. Arrows began to buzz through the air, thicker than flies on a fish-heap. Every Dragon who raised a paw in anger dropped dead to the stone floor. But the monks, who stood beside them escaped unharmed.

Some of the Dragons began to cry out, saying that

The Great Archer had come down from the stars to take them on the Wild Hunt.

'Run heathens!' growled Hardlarder in amazement. 'Get gone from this place before his servant takes his revenge on all of you.'

The Dragons that still lived ran for their lives. They poured from the chronicle house like rats down a sewer-pipe, carrying the stricken body of their wicked old leader on their backs.

Arnuf untied the rope from Billi's throat.

'Father?' cried the goat.

'Archer?' gasped Arnuf as a tall shape stepped out of the shadows. 'Where did you spring from?'

Then I realised.

'He's been on our trail for weeks,' I said. 'He followed us to the Farne Islands and back.'

'Ye ken well,' said the Archer, his voice scraping like a spear on a grind-stone.

'That arrow in the sand,' I cried. 'That was you. And the Helscaps on the hermit's island. And the guards...'

'Now I have ye – lone wolf!' he replied.

'Spill no more blood in this house, I beg you,' said Brother Goodoldboyson.

'Fear not Fathers, I will nae harm ye. But as for this flesh-eater... he cannae live.'

Arnuf let out a howl and sank to the ground.

'Not ye,' said the Archer. 'Ye spoke up for my son.'

'I was going to speak up too,' I lied. 'I was about to plead for Billi's life but you started shooting and I... er forgot.'

The Archer smiled a grim smile and shook his head. Then he strung a dart to his bow and bent back the string. I began to tremble. His arrow had Beowuff's name on it! I might just have well have tried pleading with a slab of granite.

'Stay your paw Archer!' begged Fastwagger. 'Three times we have begged Beowuff to help us and thrice he has put himself in harm's way to save the monastery.'

The Archer stood still as a rune-stone in a rainstorm.

'I speak the truth, don't I Brothers?' called Fastwagger.

The pack of monks muttered their approval. Some of them even began to chant again. I wished they'd shut up. Then I realised that they were praying for me.

'He speaks the truth,' said Billi. 'I was nae kidnapped. I begged them tae take me to see Gutland.'

The Archer shook his horned head.

'Son, Beowuff is a flesh-eater. He'll tak life without need. The world is better wi one less who lives by killing.'

I thought this was a bit rich, coming from one who decorates his hut with wolf-heads, but I decided to keep my clever mouth shut.

'He's not eaten meat for three weeks,' said Fastwagger.

The Archer lowered his bow for a moment.

'Monks! Who is yer leader?' he demanded.

I pointed out Brother Goodoldboyson, but Hardlarder

stepped forward in a lordly manner. My gut-sack began to shake. My fate was in the paws of a hard-bitten old sour-snout who hated me from nose to tail.

'Monk-father,' demanded the Archer. 'Have ye seen this lone-wolf ganging after flesh?'

Old Hardlarder made a great show of scratching his ears as he thought long and hard.

I knew that he was enjoying my torment.

'You can trust the words of our Abbot, archer,' said Fastwagger. 'He is the leader of our Order and to speak an untrue word is an offense against our sacred law.'

'When he first came amongst us, Beowuff wanted to punish the meat-plate,' said Hardlarder in a grave voice. The Archer let out a snort of disgust and drew back his bowstring ready to fire.

'I remember that Beowuff had carrion breath and an unclean reek of flesh about him...'

'D'ya ken that son?' cried the Archer. 'I told ye he was evil.'

He drew back the bow. 'Look away now Brothers. Look away child!'

'Hold!' called Hardlarder in a voice like thunder. 'I cannot tell a lie. No meat has passed Beowuff's mouth since he returned to us. I suppose that has tried to help us against the Dragon Raiders, in his own manner.'

The Archer let out a sigh and lowered his bow.

'It seems I've misjudged ye... Beowuff,' he said.

'Probably not,' muttered Hardlarder.

CHAPTER TWENTY-ONE

THE HAMMER AND THE CROSS

Setting off down the track, I looked out across the bay. The sea was puddle-smooth and grey as goose wings under the moon. A red deer leapt out and danced down the road ahead of me, but I did not chase it.

The warm wind rustled my heavy woollen robe.

Curse that Archer! He had made it a condition that I must join up with the monk-pack. It was a choice between promising to live as a prayer-sayer or taking an arrow through the heart, so I chose the former.

'Curse these itching monk-cloaks,' I muttered. 'The Brothers must knit them out of gnat's teeth.'

'Hello,' called Arnuf.

We came upon a lonely figure, up to his knees in muck and dirt.

'Brother Beowuff?' barked Hardlarder. I knew he was pleased to see me by the way he screwed up his snout.

'Digging ditches Abbot?' I said in surprise.

'I am not the Abbot now,' he said wearily. 'As well you know, young Fastwagger is taking his turn.'

'We know,' said Arnuf. 'He has sent us out upon the road. We will do good and help the poor and wherever we go. For now the two of us are- cormorants.'

'What?' growled Hardlarder in surprise.

'Mendicants Arnuf,' I corrected. 'Cormorants are

fish-eating seabirds. Mendicants are travelling monks.'

'Oh!' said Arnuf. 'Sorry.'

'Off you fly then,' growled an irritated Hardlarder, turning back to his diggings.

As we walked down the track, he looked up.

'Remember that someone is always watching over you. Let that be a comfort – to you both,' he called.

'As for me,' I replied, 'it is no great comfort to think that someone is watching me. I would rather slip through life unseen.'

But my voice was lost on the wind and the old prayer-sayer did not reply. I turned to Arnuf.

'What about you pew-mate? After we escaped so many dangers did you think you were in the care of someone great and powerful?'

'I always knew it,' he replied.

'But how can you be so... sure Arnuf?' I asked.

In a way, I envied my bench-mate, for being so certain. It must have made our trials easier.

He fixed me with a serious stare.

'I was sure we'd come through, because I have these...'

From inside his cloak he drew out his old wooden cross-sticks and touched them for luck.

'Abbot Fastwagger will be delighted,' I said.

'And if they should ever fail me,' he said seriously, 'I also have this.'

He opened his other paw to reveal his little silver Thor's hammer.

'Better to be saved than sorry,' he said.

BEOWUFF
and THE
Horrid HEN

Viking dog Beowuff is all bark and no bite, a disgrace to the memory of his fierce ancestors. Banished from his homeland (for looting his Lord's bone hoard) he finds himself shipwrecked on a troubled island. Its King needs a champion. His Great Feasting Kennel is under attack from the hideous Hendel – an evil chicken of monstrous proportions. Can Beowuff save the day?

Some of Beowuff's adventures might sound familiar to history lovers, because they echo the ancient tale of Beowulf (1000 A.D.), one of the earliest recorded poems in Old English.

ISBN: 9781906132385
UK £7.99
USA $14.95/ CAN $16.95

"My husband, professor Burns Longship has made a second incredible find! This time there are dragons involved as well as Viking dogs! Surely now the experts in Scandinavia will return my calls!"
– Mrs Burns-Longship, The Village Blog.

www.mogzilla.co.uk/beowuff

I AM SPARTAPUSS

By Robin Price

In the first adventure in the Spartapuss series...
Rome AD 36. The mighty Feline Empire rules the world.
Spartapuss, a ginger cat is comfortable managing Rome's
finest Bath and Spa. But Fortune has other plans for him.
Spartapuss is arrested and imprisoned by Catligula, the
Emperor's heir. Sent to a school for gladiators, he must fight
and win his freedom in the Arena – before his opponents
make dog food out of him.

'This witty Roman romp is history with cattitude.'
Junior Magazine (Scholastic)

ISBN 13: 978-0-9546576-0-4
UK £7.99
USA $14.95/ CAN $16.95

The Spartapuss Series:

I Am Spartapuss (Book I)
Catligula (Book II)
Die Clawdius (Book III)
Boudicat (Book IV)
Cleocatra's Kushion (Book V)

www.mogzilla.co.uk/spartapuss

CATLIGULA

By Robin Price

'Was this the most unkindest kit of all?'

In the second adventure in the Spartapuss series...

Catligula becomes Emperor and his madness brings Rome to within a whisker of disaster. When Spartapuss gets a job at the Imperial Palace, Catligula wants him as his new best friend. The Spraetorian Guard hatch a plot to destroy this power-crazed puss in an Arena ambush. Will Spartapuss go through with it, or will our six-clawed hero become history?

ISBN 9780954657611
UK £7.99
USA $14.95/ CAN $16.95

www.mogzilla.co.uk/spartapuss

In the first *London Deep* adventure...

Jemima Mallard is having a bad day. First she loses her air, then someone steals her houseboat, and now the Youth Cops think she's mixed up with a criminal called Father Thames. Not even her dad, a Chief Inspector with the 'Dult Police, can help her out this time. Oh – and London's still sinking. It's been underwater ever since the climate upgrade.

ISBN: 978-1-906132-03-3 £7.99

www.mogzilla.co.uk/londondeep

Chosen as a 'Recommended Read' for World Book Day 2011.
One of the *Manchester Book Award's* 24 recommended titles for. 2010.

MOGZILLA

ABOUT THE TRANSLATOR

Professor Burns-Longship is the translator of the *Beowuff* sagas. He speaks five languages (three of them 'dead' and one on its last legs). Despite his widely reported spat with Dr Sven Smugaxe of the Stockholm Institute of Vikingology, Professor Burns-Longship is still generally acknowledged to be the world's leading authority on Viking dogs. He lives and works in the charming village of Wuffton-Basset, although his field-trips take him everywhere from Oxford to Oslo. When not translating Beowuff sagas, he writes for *The Village Blog*.